A Royal Ruse

THE REBECCA ORANGE CASTLE COZY MYSTERY SERIES

BOOK THREE

VALERIE BRANDY

❀ Created with Vellum

Contents

CHAPTER

One

I KIND OF UNDERSTAND WHY *people become monks, now,* I think to myself as I take in the glinting stained glass windows of the rebuilt monastery that cradles me in its arms. I'm standing in an ancient building that used to house spiritual leaders, but that's now been renovated for a modern purpose. I appreciate that the building has been allowed to keep its original charm. Stone walls frame archways, butting up against firm, wooden doors with iron locks. It's a place that *would* be peaceful if it weren't currently swimming with visitors.

I lean down to my dog, Joe— who's standing by my side — and scratch his enormous, golden head. He's dressed for the occasion, wearing a bandana that cascades down his chest. It's printed with the image of a suit on it, and when he sits down, he looks like he's in formal clothes. "What do you think, bud?" I ask him. "You were bred for this. Could *you* live in a monastery?"

"You already have a castle!" Maggie laughs beside me, swishing around in her sequined dress. "What more do you two want?" She pauses as a waiter comes by, holding a plate of hors d'oeuvres. She grabs a pastry wrapped in bacon off the plate and shoves it in her mouth, taking another sip of her wine. "I wish the Duke would start his speech already," she says, mouth full. "I have so much work to do for the grand opening—"

Just then, a crackling noise emerges from a platform that's been set up as a stage at the front of the monastery's enormous grand hall. In front of us, the entire village has assembled, eager townsfolk awaiting to hear what's planned for this building— straight from Jack, the Duke of Atwood. He stands at the microphone, arms open wide.

"Welcome," says the Duke. "I'm so glad you could all make it." Jack's voice makes my stomach fill with butterflies. I try to ignore them. Jack is my boss and falling in love with him is a terrible idea. *Keep it professional, Rebecca,* I think. To distract myself, I look around at the crowd that's assembled under the elaborate arches and exposed stonework. The entire town seems to have turned out.

"Welcome to our town preview of the new Royal Heritage Museum! You are the very first to see it," The Duke continues proudly. "The monastery hasn't been used in hundreds of years, and we thought there was no better way to honor its history than to renovate the space and give it back to the people as a museum."

Typical Jack, I can't help but smile. He always wants to give back to the town and its residents— even when it costs him personally.

"In addition to displaying items from the Village of Atwood's history, I'm thrilled to announce that this museum will soon house the pride and joy of Monrovia's past…" Jack pauses for dramatic effect. "The Monrovian Crown Jewels."

Gasps emerge from the crowd. A ripple of excitement fills the hall. I turn to Maggie, who beams at me. She can tell by my expression I don't understand the excitement. "It's a very big deal, Rebecca," she whispers. "The Monrovian Crown Jewels are our most famous historical artifact. They've never been put on public display before. Bringing the jewels here is a huge honor for the Village of Atwood."

"I'd like to offer special thanks to our museum curator, Dr. Lauda Remier, who recently graduated with her PhD from the Monrovian Institute, and has personally ensured our museum exhibitions live up to the highest of standards." The Duke motions to a woman standing off to the side of the stage. She's homely-looking, wearing a suit jacket and glasses, her dark hair pulled back into a tight bun. She waves at the crowd.

"Tonight, I'm pleased to show you the interior of the museum, and encourage you to take in our exhibits, including ancient Monrovian pottery," Jack continues, waving at the space. "Tomorrow morning, you'll get a sneak preview of the Crown Jewels in the town square at a special event *just* for Atwood locals. After that, we'll hold a museum grand opening— a big event to announce this to the world. Once the rest of the world knows, I'm afraid the museum will be packed with tourists, so I'd like to give the townsfolk first chance at seeing the gems tomorrow." Murmurs of approval ripple through the room. "If everything goes as planned, the museum will bring millions of tourist dollars to the Village of Atwood, as well as to our small businesses here, like *Le Petite Scone,*" the Duke motions to the baker, Henri, who's standing at the front of the crown, still wearing his white chef's uniform. "Or *Cafe de Flore,*" Jack adds, waving to Jocelyn, the owner of my favorite cafe in town. "My hope is that every business in the village will see new opportunities for growth, given the increase in tourism brought by making Atwood the home of the Crown Jewels. But we can't do this without you," the Duke adds, meeting people's eyes. I see nods all around me— the townspeople are already sold on the idea. "The increase in visitors will mean changes in Atwood, but also new opportunity. And we're going to tackle it as we always do… together."

As Jack's speech ends, the room erupts into thunderous applause. The crown returns to their snacks and mingling as Jack descends from the stage, shaking hands as he goes.

"He's really going all in," I whisper to Maggie. Joe is busy weaving between my legs, thrilled by the crowd and attention.

"He wants this more than anything," she says, squeezing my arm. "He thinks it will give the economy here a boost. Looks like everyone thinks so, too."

I scan the room. There's Benjamin, the owner of *L'animalerie Indiana Bones* talking a mile a minute to a village, most likely about his favorite movies. Henri the baker looks especially pleased, like he knows exactly how many pastries this will sell. Jocelyn and Zacharia— the new owner of the gossip magazine stand— are leaning toward each other, deep in conversation. At the far end of the room, I see Castle Atwood staff standing in a circle, looking thrilled at the news. Everyone seems swept up by the announcement.

Maggie leans in closer. "There she is," she says, nodding to the stage. I spot a young woman in towering heels and trendy clothes, barely containing her boredom. She shakes Jack's hand as he walks off the stage, but looks like she'd rather be anywhere else. "Lady Henrietta Grendana," Maggie explains. "And the little one next to her is her lady in waiting, Bitty. They've been awful guests at the castle. Poor Monique had to clean their room three times until it was to their liking, and Enrique's exhausted from driving them all around town." I glance back at the Castle Atwood staff, and notice that Monique and Enrique *do* look particularly tired, leaning up against each other in hushed conversation.

Just then, the Duke approaches, and time seems to slow down as he walks toward me. *Try to look like a normal human being, Rebecca,* I say to myself. *Close your mouth. Don't hold it open like a trout.* I shut my mouth and swirl my drink in its glass, offering the Duke a soft smile. I hate that I've grown to like my boss so much, but funny enough, it's for all the right reasons. I don't care about his Royal title or family money. I just like the way he spends nights at the library, and the crinkle in his smile.

"Do you two think it went well?" The Duke asks Maggie and I in a hushed tone, glancing around the room.

"They loved it," I assure him. "That was some speech you made."

"This is going to change *everything*," Maggie says, jumping up and down. "Atwood will be busier than ever this summer."

"*Oui*," a gruff voice says over Maggie's shoulder. It belongs to Henri, who's as close to 'happy' as I've ever seen him. Henri doesn't smile much, but there's crumbs in his beard, and his eyes are lit up. "I may finally be able to hire more help," he says. "No more hand-rolling croissants for me."

The Duke puts a hand on Henri's shoulder as if they're old friends. "Henri has promised me a small favor. Actually, it's a favor for you *and* me, Rebecca," he adds, the slightest flush coloring his cheeks.

"Yes, yes," Henri says, waving a hand in the air. "*Le Petite Scone* is yours for an evening. I will keep the staff late. Draw the blinds. No one will be the wiser."

My heart pounds in my chest. I was sure the Duke had forgotten the dinner he'd promised, but here he is, arranging everything. Whenever I think he's forgotten all about me, he proves otherwise.

"This weekend, Rebecca. You and me. A night with no crowds and no interruptions. What do you say?" Jacks smiles at me.

"Only if Joe can come," I say stupidly, acting as if my dog is an emotional support animal.

"I wouldn't expect anything else," Jack agrees. Then, he

looks around the room. "Where *is* the little rascal? I would think he'd be here in full regalia."

I glance down, realizing Joe has disappeared. Then, a hand waves at me from the other side of the grand hall. It's Benjamin, and he's feeding Joe snacks from off his plate. He points to Joe's outfit and gives me a thumbs up. We bought the attire from Benjamin's store, and it seems as if he approves.

"Looks like I was right," the Duke smiles. "I'd better get back to my guests," he adds, looking back at Lady Henrietta, who's still standing by the stage. "I don't know if Maggie's told you but my extended family is…"

"Evil—" Maggie interjects.

"*Difficult,*" the Duke smirks. "Rebecca, I look forward to this weekend."

The Duke offers a polite kiss on my hand before heading back toward the stage. Maggie offers me a knowing grin.

"Don't say a word—" I caution her.

"Wasn't going to!"

"Royalty and—" Henri scoffs, scanning me head to toe. "And ordinary person. What can it be?"

"Henri!" Maggi says, slapping his arm.

"I know, I know," I say, familiar with Henri's prejudice. "I'm American and I couldn't possibly understand."

"*Non,* it's not that you are American," Henri says, shaking his head. "It's that you are as ordinary as Maggie and me. These Royals, they live in a different world." He points at the Duke, who's standing beside Lady Henrietta, both of them looking other-worldly in their formal attire. "They are groomed for the crown. They can never understand the ordinary person, nor can an ordinary person understand them. You work with animals, yes? Then you must know, a bird and a fish can never be."

"That's great Henri," Maggie says, rolling her eyes. "But

we have to stop Rebecca's dog from eating ice out of that champagne bucket."

"Blame me if you must," Henri says, throwing his hands in the air. "But I am only speaking the truth. Look at how the Crown Jewels came to be. Even when the commoner has money, it does not matter— love *cannot* overcome all."

"Thanks for the pep talk, but we'll be going now!" Maggie says. She grabs my elbow and pulls me across the room. Henri's voice echoes in my ears. *A bird and a fish can never be.* It's never occurred to me before that my lack of Royal status might be a problem in dating the Duke. I'd been so obsessed with the idea he's my boss, it hadn't even hit me we might have a bigger issue — he's *Royal.* And I'm— just Rebecca Orange. *An animal trainer with messy hair and a midnight ice-cream habit,* I think to myself.

"Rebecca," Maggie clucks at me, shaking her head. She can see the pain that's etched in my eyes. "Henri is an idiot. We keep him around because he makes amazing croissants, but he's an idiot with outdated ideas. Don't let him get to you."

"But what if he's right?"

"He's *never* right," Maggie sighs. "Unless it comes to bread. Then he's usually right. But everything else? He's an idiot. He once told me I was improper for using the castle SUV to pickup my breakfast and that the car should be for Royals only. I was so mad I almost revoked his business license, but then I remembered that little bread he makes with the golden raisins. You know that one?"

"I know it *too* well," I say.

"And I just couldn't revoke his license out of vengeance," she sighs. "Mostly because it's wrong, but also because I *need* that raisin bread for survival. But the point is— don't listen to anything Henri says."

She pulls me toward Joe, who— as Maggie correctly pointed out— has gotten into the ice box under the bar, where bottles of champagne are being kept. I grab him by the collar and he emerges, chewing a giant ice cube and crunching it right in front of me. "Joe," I laugh. "You are the world's *worst*, *best*-trained dog."

His eyebrows arch at me, softening the sting of our exchange with Henri. Still, the idea's been planted, and I wonder once again if my upcoming dinner with Jack is really a date, or just a warm friendship. Even if it *is* a date, maybe the Duke only sees me as someone to bide the time with, rather than someone to love.

"I think I might call it a night," I say to Maggie, secretly hoping to get back to my apartment at the castle and dip into my giant bathtub.

"Me too," Maggie yawns, checking her watch. "I've got so much to do tomorrow."

The three of us move to leave together, making our way toward the entrance. The old monastery doors are thrown wide open. A gentle breeze carries the sound of festivities into the evening. Just when I think we might escape, Joe puts on the brakes. He's focused on a tall man standing just outside the doorway. The man's got a gun at his side, but Joe's far more interested in the snack peeking from his pocket. He drags me over to investigate. "Looks like someone needs a treat," the man says in a thick Monrovian accent, offering a chunk of pastry to my giant dog. "Or maybe you're looking for a job?"

The man's grinning, broad and muscular with the air of someone who doesn't scare easily. He holds out a hand in greeting, and I shake it. "I'm Anthony, with the Royal Guard," he says.

"Anthony's in charge of protecting the jewels," Maggie adds. "The Royal Family sent him specifically to look after them."

"I could use some help, though," Anthony smiles at Joe. "Any chance your dog would want to join me as backup?"

"Trust me, you don't want him," I laugh. "If a jewel thief offers him some bacon, those gems are gone."

Anthony offers a hearty laugh as we depart, waving at us as we head down the steps. The night air is brisk and cool. The monastery is located on the edge of the village near a peaceful road. The cobblestones click under my feet as the moon lights the way. Then, the silence is interrupted by a woman's voice.

We *hear* the protestor before we see her, and I can just make out the sign in her hand. "Keep your jewels! Royals are wrong!" She shouts her chant against the night, her figure pacing in place as a lone bastion to her cause. "Royals are wrong! Royals are wrong!"

"Oh *no*," Maggie lets out a low whistler. "Well, at least it's only one..."

We approach the protestor, and I get a better look at her under the light escaping through the open monastery doors. She's a young woman in her early twenties with with electric blue hair. She's holding a sign above her head, but she sets it down on our approach, and grabs a pamphlet out of her pocket. "Take one?" she asks.

"What exactly are you protesting?" I say, grabbing the pamphlet and opening it up to find a picture of the Royal Family within.

"The Crown Jewels are a symbol of monarchical oppression," the woman says passionately.

"Thanks but no thanks," Maggie rolls her eyes. "That monarchical oppression pays *both* our salaries." Maggie proceeds to continue her walk down the cobblestone path, and Joe and I follow her.

"If you change your mind, my email is on there!" The woman shouts behind us. "Pepper dot anarchist!"

"Pepper dot anarchist?" I whisper to Maggie under my breath, laughing. "Our big opposition is one girl named Pepper who doesn't believe in any sort of government at all?"

"At least it's not an angry mob," Maggie agrees. "I just hope she's not at the grand unveiling of the jewels tomorrow. We really need this to go to smoothly. The Duke, the castle, the village… we're all counting on this. It's a new world, and the village needs tourists to stay afloat."

"Maggie," I say, shaking my head. "It's *us*. When do we ever find things go smoothly?

Maggie laughs and— with perfect timing— Joe lets out an enormous sigh, as if he's certain trouble is just on the horizon and even the idea of it is exhausting him. I scratch his ears, bending down to his level.

"What do you think, bud? Will things go smoothly tomorrow?" I ask him.

His big, soft eyes say no. And a glance back at Pepper— still marching in place— tells me he's right.

CHAPTER
Two

LATER, Maggie, Joe, and I meet again at the castle's staff dining hall for a meal. Dinner is another feast, and Chef Renauld outdoes herself. The pasta melts in my mouth, a pink cream sauce rich enough to make me want seconds. Or thirds. I can barely make out Maggie through the massive bouquet of wildflowers at the center of the table, but I catch her eyes and smile. Joe is underfoot, munching on a piece of liver made special just for him. The dining quarters buzz with talk about the museum opening, everyone chattering over each other in excitement. "I arranged for press from all over Monrovia," Maggie says, pushing the flowers aside so she can see me from across the table. Tonight, she's more interested in gossip than pasta.

She's about to say something else, but Douglas, the groundskeeper, interrupts from down the table. "You better keep Joe out of the gardens this week, Rebecca," he says, squinting at me with mock seriousness. "He did quite the number on the chrysanthemums last time."

"Douglas, he was helping!" I reply, watching as Joe licks his bowl clean and starts eying the leftovers on my plate. "You should see how great his pruning skills are."

Maggie laughs and scoops up more pasta, barely missing a beat. "Isn't this sauce amazing?" She twirls her fork in the air, almost losing a noodle to gravity. "I could eat it every night."

Tracey, our resident fitness instructor, arches an eyebrow. "You *will* eat it every night, if you're not careful. Remember what we talked about at our last session, Maggie? Moderation?" Despite Tracey's protest, I notice she's not having one of her traditional green smoothies tonight, and is instead indulging in Chef's pasta. Even Tracey can't resist tonight's meal.

"Oh, please!" Maggie says with a grin. "No amount fitness *feels* as good as this pasta *tastes*."

Someone— I can't see who through all the flowers — shouts out: "I've waited my whole life to see those gems! Is it true they're worth ten million dollars?"

"Is it?" I whisper to Maggie.

She shrugs. "I don't know. I've never had them appraised. But I expect they're priceless. Reporters from around the country are coming into town tomorrow to document the unveiling, so I'm sure there will be speculation in the press about what they're worth. I promised Zacharia ten minutes alone with the Duke, given that he's our resident gossip columnist."

"I get that these are the Crown Jewels, but besides that, what makes them so news-worthy?"

"The history," Maggie replies, pushing her empty plate away. "The jewels represent Monrovia itself. They are the heart of our country. Long ago," she says, dropping her voice like we're at a campfire telling ghost stories, "there was a Monrovian queen who loved a rich merchant. A commoner. Every time he went on a voyage, he brought her back larger and larger gifts from all over the world. Exotic clothes... Spices..."

"I get what the Queen saw in him," I say. "Bringing her gifts all the time? I think *I'm* in love with him."

Maggie laughs. "The merchant was clearly a lovable guy, I agree. And when he returned from his second-to-last trip, he brought the Queen the Crown Jewels... and *proposed* marriage. The Queen was moved. Deeply moved. But she declined because she thought it would destroy the Monrovian monarchy to marry a commoner."

"But why would that destroy the monarchy?" I interrupt, unable to keep the personal offense out of my voice.

"Because," Maggie explains, giving me a pointed look, "monarchies thrive on bloodlines. The Queen was worried that if she married outside her station, her children might not have a claim on the throne."

"And so?"

"And so... she turned him down," Maggie says, her voice dropping to an appropriately tragic tone. "But it gets worse."

The table has quieted now, everyone listening in as if Maggie is the world's best storybook reader. I hear Tracey whisper to Douglas: "Isn't this story *so* romantic?"

"No," he whispers back. "Not when the guy gets rejected!"

Maggie pretends not to notice the side conversation and forges ahead. "After the Queen's rejection, the merchant went on another voyage— his most dangerous yet— and was lost at sea. Most likely, he was killed in a storm. His ship was never found, but news of his disappearance was brought back to the Queen. The Queen was so heartbroken and regretted her decision *so* much that she made the jewels the Crown Jewels, representative of the country of Monrovia. And they've been that ever since."

The room buzzes with noise again as the story ends. Joe gives me a hopeful nudge with his nose, and I reward him with a bit of pasta that's more sauce than noodle. Maggie watches with a smirk and asks: "Well? What do you think?"

"I think," I say slowly, pretending to savor the bite, "you and Henri tell the same story."

"No, we don't," Maggie shakes her head. "If that's what you think you're missing the point, Rebecca!"

"I'm not worried about Henri. I'm worried about what the story means today. If this were happening now, would a queen feel the same way? Would it still be the end of the world to marry a commoner?"

Maggie tilts her head, considering. "It wouldn't be easy," she admits, softening her voice so it's lost to everyone but me. "But the Crown Jewels have meant so much for so long. Seeing them on display tomorrow—well, I can't wait for you to experience it. Maybe you'll see what the story of the jewels really means."

I nod, not entirely convinced, but Joe's happy face makes up for it.

When dinner is finished, Joe and I stroll through the cool night air, the castle grounds quiet except for our footsteps. I've got leftover pasta for Alfredo and need to check that all the animals are tucked in for the night. I pause by the menagerie, calling to Alfredo as Joe sniffs at the empty feed buckets. "Pasta!" I call out, holding up the carton of leftovers. "Leftover pink cream sauce for one hungry giraffe!"

I spot Alfredo's long neck stretching over the fence. He knows a good deal when he sees one.

"This is your lucky night," I say, scooping some into his feed bin. "Chef Renauld's finest. I shouldn't share, but I can't resist your charming spots." I can't help but wonder at the fact that when I started at the castle, I was completely opposed to feeding the giraffe pasta. Now, he's won me over.

Alfredo butts his head against the gate, and Joe watches him like he might consider giraffe-chasing as a new hobby.

"Let's settle this," I say, feeling a little foolish for trying to have a heart-to-heart with an animal. "Alfredo, you were born here in Monrovia. So… what do you think? Henri says Royals can't marry commoners, even now. Do you think that's true?"

Alfredo looks at me, then at the pasta, then back at me, and I'm convinced he's on the verge of breaking his silence.

"I didn't say you had to answer right away," I tell him, as if he's chewing on something bigger than noodles.

I put a little more pasta in Alfredo's bin, and he swallows it in one massive gulp. He makes a pleased sound, then nudges me for more. I take it as a sign that he's thinking it over. Joe gives a low, not-so-pleased whine, and I sigh, splitting the last of the leftovers onto a nearby rock. "You just had dinner," I say. Joe looks back at me, suggesting second-dinner is also a meal worth enjoying. I grab the feed buckets and toss what's inside onto the grounds, watching as the zebras and alpaca approach to nibble up their meals.

While they eat, I lean against the gate, listening to the sounds of the castle at night. It's peaceful out here, which is almost enough to make me stop worrying. Almost.

"So I'm not Royal," I say, tossing a few more pellets into the enclosure. "Maybe the Duke likes me well enough, but knows it can't go anywhere."

Alfredo looks at me with those big, wondering eyes, and I imagine him saying: Who knows? I'm just a giraffe.

Then, right on cue, he sneezes. The wet contents of his nose splash across my face.

Joe lets out a bark like he's laughing, and I wipe my face with the back of my hand.

"You make a good point, Alfredo," I say, staring up at the giraffe "Maybe we should just see the Crown Jewels before we think ourselves silly."

Joe lets out a final bark that sounds suspiciously like agreement, and we head back through the quiet grounds. Tomorrow will be here soon enough, with or without answers.

CHAPTER
Three

IT'S MORNING, and the Atwood town square sparkles like it's been polished just for today. Medieval stone buildings frame the central fountain where water catches the light. Streamers in Monrovia's national colors flutter between lamp posts. Joe sits obediently at my side, though his massive frame draws stares. Life in Monrovia never stops feeling like a surprise, and I still can't believe I'm here—standing among castle staff for the grand unveiling of the Crown Jewels. It's like I've stumbled into a fairy tale.

"Quite the turnout," I say to Maggie, who's checking something on her tablet while simultaneously straightening her jacket.

"The entire village turned out," Maggie murmurs, scanning the growing throng of people. "And half of Europe's press is here."

She's not exaggerating. The square is packed with journalists clutching cameras and notepads, tourists with their phones held high, and locals who've closed their shops for the morning to witness history. At the center of it all stands an elegant cart draped with thick red fabric, presumably concealing the legendary Crown Jewels beneath. Museum staff hurry about, making last-minute adjustments to the setup.

I spot familiar faces in the crowd—Benjamin from the pet shop waves enthusiastically when he catches my eye. His "L'animalerie Indiana Bones" shop has become Joe's favorite stop on our morning walks, largely because Benjamin always has premium treats waiting.

"Rebecca! Hello!" he calls out, making his way toward us. "I closed the shop today. This is bigger than selling dog toys, no?" His slight French accent makes even the most mundane statements sound charming.

"Definitely bigger," I agree with a smile. "Joe was disappointed to miss his morning visit, though."

Benjamin crouches down to Joe's level, earning an appreciative tail wag. "Ah, my friend! Don't worry, I brought you something." He produces a dog biscuit from his pocket, looking to me for permission before offering it. I nod, and Joe delicately takes the treat with surprising gentleness for a dog his size.

"Have you seen Jocelyn today?" I ask, scanning the crowd for the café owner.

"She's over there," Benjamin points toward Café de Flore's proprietor, who stands near the fountain with a thermos. "She's giving free coffee samples to promote the café. Smart woman."

Jocelyn catches us looking and offers a small wave.

"I should get back to my spot," Benjamin says. "I want to see the jewels up close! They say the tiara alone is worth ten million dollars!"

As he disappears into the crowd, I notice Zacharia darting between groups of people, camera in hand. The young apprentice from the local newsstand looks like he's living his dream today, rubbing elbows with professional photographers. Since his mentor Rodrigo passed away, he's been determined to prove himself worthy of taking over the newsstand permanently.

"Here they come," Maggie whispers, straightening her posture.

A hush falls over the crowd as the Duke of Atwood approaches the stage, followed by Lady Henrietta, who looks flawless in white skirt and top. Her carefully arranged features wear an expression of practiced boredom, while her lady-in-waiting—Bitty, I believe Maggie called her—trails behind, phone at the ready as if waiting for the perfect Instagram moment. The museum curator, Lauda, walks alongside them, smiling behind her glasses.

The Duke steps onto the small platform, looking every inch a Royal in a tailored navy suit with subtle Monrovian emblems on the lapels.

"Good morning, everyone," he begins, his voice carrying easily across the square without need of the microphone set before him. "What a wonderful day for Atwood and all of Monrovia."

The crowd murmurs in agreement. Joe sits perfectly still beside me, as if he too understands the significance of the moment.

"Today marks a new chapter in our nation's relationship with its history," the Duke continues. "For centuries, the Crown Jewels have been tucked away, symbols of privilege viewed by only a select few. But now, we make them available to the public."

A smattering of applause breaks out. I notice Lady Henrietta examining her manicure with exaggerated interest while Bitty snaps candid photos of her.

"I must extend my deepest gratitude to my cousin, Lady Henrietta Grendana," the Duke says, turning toward the young woman, "for allowing these treasures to leave their home at Grendana Castle and for personally escorting them here today."

Lady Henrietta offers a slight nod, the barest acknowledgment of the crowd's attention. Bitty leans in to whisper something that makes her smirk.

"It's a small sacrifice," Lady Henrietta replies in a bored tone that suggests it's anything but small. "Grandmother insisted I show support for the... common touch."

The Duke's smile doesn't falter, but I catch a brief tightening around his eyes before he smoothly turns his attention elsewhere.

"I would also like to acknowledge another passionate Monrovian," he says, gesturing to the side of the square where Pepper— the young woman with blue hair has— handcuffed herself to a lamp post. Protest signs lean against the post, bearing slogans about wealth redistribution and the evils of monarchy.

"No to Monarchy!" She shouts. "Resist, you fools!"

The crowd turns to look, some with frowns, others with curious expressions.

"Pepper has been here since dawn," the Duke says with unexpected warmth in his voice, "exercising her civic right to protest what she sees as an unjust system."

Pepper looks momentarily thrown by the acknowledgment, then raises her free hand in a defiant gesture that makes several people laugh.

"While Pepper and I may disagree on the best path forward," the Duke continues, "I deeply respect her commitment to creating a more equitable Monrovia. That passion for positive change makes her, in my view, an excellent role model for all Monrovians."

Typical Jack, I think. The fact that he isn't intimidated by people who disagree with him makes him even *more* attractive.

The Duke gestures to the woman beside him. "I'll now turn things over to Lauda, our brilliant museum curator, who can tell you more about the historical significance of what you're about to see."

Lauda steps forward, adjusting her glasses with slightly trembling hands. Her voice, when she speaks, is steady and authoritative despite her obvious nerves.

"The Crown Jewels of Monrovia tell a story of love and loss that transcends their monetary value," she begins. "The collection was gifted to Queen Eleanora III by a man who loved her deeply but could never marry her due to his common birth."

The crowd leans in, captivated by the romance of it all.

"After his death at sea, the Queen was so consumed by grief that she declared the jewels to be the official crown jewels of Monrovia, ensuring his memory would live on as symbol of what Monrovia truly stands for. Today marks the first time in over a century that these treasures will be on public display," Lauda concludes. "I'm honored to curate this collection, and we at the Royal Heritage Museum are pleased to make them accessible to all Monrovians and visitors."

The Duke steps forward again, moving toward the draped case.

"Without further ado," the Duke announces, his hand reaching for the red fabric, "I present to you, the Crown Jewels of Monrovia!"

He pulls the cloth away with a flourish. The crowd collectively inhales, cameras flash—and then there's silence. Pure, stunned silence.

The display case is *empty*.

I blink, certain I must be missing something. The glass case sits pristinely on the cart, lights positioned to illuminate treasures that aren't there. No diamond tiara. No ruby heart necklace. No diamond ring. No pearl bracelet. Nothing.

The silence stretches for three long seconds before exploding into chaos.

"Where are they?" someone shouts.

"They've been stolen!" calls another voice.

Camera flashes intensify as journalists surge forward. The guards immediately form a tighter perimeter around the empty case, though it's clearly too late for such precautions.

Lady Henrietta sways slightly, her face drained of color. "I told Grandmother sharing the jewels with commoners was a terrible idea," she hisses to Bitty, who looks equally shocked but manages to steady her employer.

Lauda stares at the empty case, her mouth opening and closing without sound. When she finally speaks, her voice is barely audible over the growing commotion. "I apologize. We seem to have an— unexpected— situation…"

From her lamp post, Pepper lets out a whoop of delight. "The people have reclaimed what's rightfully theirs!" she shouts, rattling her handcuffs triumphantly.

The Duke maintains his composure remarkably well, though I catch the momentary flash of disbelief in his eyes before he raises his hands, calling for calm.

"Please, everyone! Step back and allow us to assess the situation."

Joe presses against my leg, sensing the shift in energy. His massive body tenses slightly, prepared to protect me if the crowd's mood turns dangerous. I place my hand on his head, both to reassure him and to ground myself.

"How could this happen?" Maggie whispers, her voice cracking. "The jewels were under constant supervision! Anthony was on duty all night."

The Duke strides through the guards toward us, his expression grave. "Maggie, Rebecca—you saw Anthony last night, correct? How did everything seem?"

"Completely normal," I reply.

"We need to find him at once—" the Duke starts to say, but he's cut off by a scream from the direction of the museum. We all turn to see a young woman in a museum uniform running toward us, her face streaked with tears.

"Your Grace!" she cries out, stumbling to a halt before the Duke. "We found—" She gasps for breath. "In the men's bathroom—it's Anthony—"

"Anthony?" the Duke asks, his voice sharp with sudden alarm.

The woman's face crumples. "He's unconscious, Your Grace. He's been hit over the head. He's breathing but only barely. We found his body locked in a stall. He'd been hit over the head. The night manager just discovered him when he went to use the facilities."

The square, already in disarray, erupts into fresh pandemonium. Parents clutch children to their sides, tourists back away from the museum, and journalists practically climb over each other to get closer to this breaking development.

Lady Henrietta lets out a small, strangled sound before Bitty whisks her toward a waiting car, photographers trailing in their wake.

The Duke turns to Maggie, his expression now steel. "Clear the square. Get an ambulance and the the police here immediately."

As Maggie rushes to comply, I feel Joe press closer to my side, his warmth a comfort against the sudden chill that's settled over me. I look at the empty display case, then toward the museum where somewhere inside lies the body of a man who just yesterday was slipping treats to my dog.

"So much for things going smoothly," Maggie mutters as she returns to my side, phone already pressed to her ear.

I nod, watching as the Duke confers with the royal guards, his posture rigid with controlled urgency. In just moments, a seemingly perfect day has transformed into something much darker.

And somehow, I have a feeling this is just the beginning.

I CAN'T BELIEVE *the Crown Jewels are missing*, I think to myself as Maggie, Joe, and I stroll across the cast courtyard. After the morning's events, the whole village was so abuzz with activity that we ran back to the castle as fast as our legs could carry us. Now, we're enjoying the sunshine that falls across the gardens, trying to make sense of everything that's happened. Joe keeps picking up on my nervous energy, staying closer to my side than usual as we wander past brightly colored flowers and vining ivy.

Maggie's been on her cellphone non-stop since this morning, reporting back as she gets new information. "The hospital says the guard in charges of the jewels— Anthony— is alive, but unconscious," Maggie says. "They're putting him on life support right now. Apparently he was hit over the head and lost quite a lot of blood."

My stomach turns, thinking about the man I'd met only a single evening prior. "He was so nice to Joe," I say, shaking my head.

She gasps, staring down at the screen. "The Duke! He didn't!"

"What?" I ask, unable to believe anything worse than the jewels being stolen could have happened.

"The Duke invited Officer Basilier to interview all the suspects here, at the castle!" Maggie says. "He's asked me to send a message to the staff to prepare the library."

"No!" I shout, making Joe whine a little. "Jack should want Officer Basilier as far away from him as possible. That woman is horrible." I shudder, remembering how she tried to blame Jack for the *last* murder that happened in Atwood.

Maggie walks on my other side, her tablet tucked under one arm as always. Even in crisis mode, her blonde braids remain perfectly in place, though I notice the worry lines between her eyebrows have deepened.

"He felt it would be better to have them come to the castle instead of the police station," she explains, glancing up from her screen. "The Duke thinks it looks more collaborative that way—like he has nothing to hide and is cooperating fully."

I snort. "That woman has made it perfectly clear she's out to get him. The man has a death wish."

We pass under a stone archway into the inner courtyard. The afternoon sun casts long shadows across the ancient cobblestones, and flower beds burst with color along the edges. After three weeks at Castle Atwood, I'm still not used to the idea that I actually live and work here. Joe, on the other hand, has adapted perfectly—prancing across the courtyard like he owns the place.

"I wish we could hear what they're saying," I mutter, looking toward the grand windows of the library where I know the interviews are taking place. "Officer Basilier will twist everyone's words to fit whatever theory she's cooked up. If we could hear what they're saying, maybe we could help."

And stop Jack from getting himself thrown in prison again, I think to myself.

Joe woofs softly in agreement, his massive tail swishing against my leg.

"You know," Maggie says slowly, a mischievous smile spreading across her face, "there might actually be a way."

She stops walking abruptly and looks at me with that spark in her eyes.

"Maggie Lefevere," I say, recognizing that look. "What are you thinking?"

"Come with me," she says, pivoting on her heel toward the east wing of the castle. "You too, Joe. He'll love this." She winks at me.

I follow her through a series of corridors until we reach one of the castle's smaller sitting rooms—the one with the built-in bookshelves that span the entire wall. It's a cozy space with deep cushioned chairs and a window seat overlooking the rose garden.

"Are we hiding in here until the interviews are over?" I ask, confused. The sitting room is lovely, but it doesn't seem like a place where we'd overhear anything useful.

"Not exactly," Maggie says, moving purposefully toward the tallest bookshelf on the far wall. "When they renovated the castle, I convinced the Duke to keep certain... historical elements intact."

She runs her fingers along the spines of several leather-bound books, then stops at a thick red volume in the center. When she pulls on it, it doesn't come out—instead, there's a soft click.

"No way," I breathe.

"Oh, there's a way," Maggie grins, pushing gently on the edge of the bookcase. It swings inward, revealing a dark passage beyond. "The castle was built in the 1500s. Of course it has secret passages."

Joe's ears perk up, his tail going into hyperdrive as he peers curiously into the darkness.

"This is... this is straight out of a movie," I say, stepping closer. "How long have you known about this?"

"Since my first week working here," Maggie admits, reaching inside to flip a switch. A string of small lights illuminates the passage. "I found the original castle plans in the archives. Most of the passages were sealed up during renovations, but I convinced them to preserve this one. For historical integrity, of course."

"Of course," I repeat, not bothering to hide my grin. "Nothing to do with being able to sneak around undetected."

"I prefer to think of it as efficient castle management," she says primly, though her eyes twinkle. "This particular passage leads behind the library. There's a one-way mirror on the other side—it looks like a regular mirror in the library, but we can see through from this side. The Duke's ancestors weren't exactly subtle with their spy craft."

"Joe?" I look down at my massive canine companion. "What do you think? Secret spy mission?"

Joe answers by stepping boldly into the passage, his tail wagging with adventure.

"I guess that's a yes," I laugh, following him in.

Maggie steps in after me and pulls the bookcase closed behind us. The passage is narrow but tall enough that we don't have to stoop. The string of soft lights gives just enough illumination to see where we're going without making it too bright. Joe leads the way, his golden coat appearing almost copper in the dim light. The walls are stone, cool to the touch, and I can feel the weight of centuries pressing in around us. Dust clings to the air, and I think about the secrets these walls could share, if they could only speak.

"Who do you think walked these passages before us?" I ask Maggie, breathless.

"The Duke's great-great-grandfather used these passages to listen in on his advisors," Maggie says. "Apparently, he caught three different assassination plots that way."

"Comforting," I mutter, ducking under a low-hanging pipe. "How much farther?"

"Just around this corner," Maggie says. "We'll come to a small chamber that backs up against the library wall."

The passage widens slightly as we turn the corner, opening into a space just large enough for the three of us. Directly in front of us is what appears to be the back of a mirror—a rectangular space in the wall covered with a semi-transparent material.

"It's a special glass," Maggie explains in a hushed voice. "From this side, we can see through it, but from the library, it just looks like a decorative mirror between the bookshelves."

I step closer and peer through. Sure enough, I can see the library beyond—a handsome room with floor-to-ceiling book-shelves, a massive fireplace, and several comfortable seating areas. The Duke stands near the fireplace, tall and distin-guished in his navy suit. His salt-and-pepper hair catches the light as he turns to speak with Officer Basilier.

The police officer looks even more severe than usual, her petite frame somehow radiating authority as she organizes a row of chairs facing the fireplace. Her uniform is impeccably pressed, and her expression suggests she'd rather be anywhere but in a royal castle.

"Perfect timing," Maggie whispers, pointing to the door where a small group of people is being escorted in. "Here come the suspects."

Joe settles at our feet with a soft huff, as if he understands the need for quiet. I scratch behind his ears absently, my attention fixed on the unfolding scene. We fall silent as the library door opens wider. From our hidden vantage point, the room itself is everything a castle library should be—rich mahogany bookshelves stretching to the ceiling, a massive stone fireplace with a gentle fire crackling despite the warm day, and plush leather chairs arranged in a semi-circle before it. If I didn't know better, I'd think this was a cozy gathering for afternoon tea, not an interrogation about missing Crown Jewels worth millions.

The Duke stands to one side of the fireplace, looking both regal and somehow approachable in his tailored navy suit. His salt-and-pepper hair is neatly combed, but a single strand has fallen across his forehead. Despite the stress of the situation, his posture remains relaxed, though I catch the slight tension around his eyes when he glances at Officer Basilier.

Officer Basilier couldn't be more his opposite. Where the Duke exudes warmth, she radiates cold authority. Though barely reaching his shoulder in height, she commands the space. Her uniform is pressed to military precision, and her short hair is equally controlled. She stands like she's ready to pounce, eyeing each person who enters as if they're already guilty.

"I feel bad that we're spying," Maggie whispers. "I hope this doesn't get me fired."

"It's not spying," I whisper back. "It's... preemptive evidence gathering."

Joe huffs softly at my feet, as if offering his own opinion on our covert operation.

The first to enter are Lady Henrietta and Bitty, practically joined at the hip. Lady Henrietta sweeps in as if she's entering a gala rather than an interrogation, her designer outfit— a white skirt and modern, white blazer—seeming wildly out of place in the historic setting. Her hair extensions cascade down her back in perfect waves, and she's wearing sunglasses indoors, which she only removes after the Duke gently clears his throat.

"Cousin Jackie-poo," she trills, moving to air-kiss the Duke's cheeks. "This is all so ridiculous, isn't it?"

Bitty, one step behind, mirrors Lady Henrietta's outfit in a slightly less expensive version, like a backup dancer to the star. She's pretty in a practiced way, with straight blonde hair and a permanent expression that suggests she's smelling something unpleasant. Her eyes dart constantly to Lady Henrietta, checking for cues on how to react.

"Where do you want us?" Lady Henrietta asks, her voice dripping with boredom.

Officer Basilier points stiffly to the couch. "Sit."

The next to enter is a stark contrast— it's Pepper, the protestor, finally freed from her handcuffs. She's wearing fishnet sleeves over her arms and dark makeup that makes her pale face even paler. Unlike the others, she enters with defiant energy, hands shoved into her pockets, eyes challenging everyone in the room.

"I have a constitutional right to a lawyer!" she says, directing the statement at the Duke rather than Officer Basilier.

The Duke smiles slightly. "This is just a preliminary conversation. But if you'd like legal representation, we can arrange that."

Pepper shrugs and drops into one of the armchairs, spreading her arms across its back as if claiming territory. "It's fine— for now. But don't test me. I know my rights."

"Duly noted," the Duke nods. "I, too, am a fan of constitutional law. If you'd like to borrow any books on the subject from our library before you leave, please, be my guest." He motions at a bookshelf against the far wall, but Pepper just huffs.

She must be fun at parties, I think, unable to believe Pepper is unmoved in the wake of the Duke's charm.

Lauda— the museum curator— enters next, walking quickly and clutching a folder to her chest like armor. In her early thirties, she looks exactly like what I'd expect from someone who works in a museum all day. She wears a simple blouse and skirt, her brown hair pulled back in a practical ponytail. Glasses perch on the bridge of her nose, and she adjusts them every few seconds.

"Thank you for coming, Dr. Lauda," the Duke says warmly.

"Of course, Your Grace," she responds, her voice steady despite her obvious nervousness. "I've brought the security logs you requested."

"Sit them on the table there," Officer Basilier cuts in, gesturing to a side table. "And then join the others."

Lauda looks surprised at his request, but she takes a seat next to Pepper, smoothing her skirt against her legs.

The last to enter is a small, slight man with a thin mustache that quivers as he dabs his forehead with a handkerchief. Despite the warm day, he's wearing a full suit, complete with a waistcoat and bow tie. He looks like he might pass out from nerves at any moment.

"Who's that?" I whisper to Maggie, pointing at the man.

"Claude, the Royal Jeweler," she whispers back. "He came with Lady Henrietta and Bitty to make sure the jewels were cared for appropriately."

"Y-Your Grace," Claude stutters, bowing deeply to the Duke. "Officer Basilier. I-I've brought the jewel maintenance records—"

"Just sit down," Officer Basilier says curtly.

With everyone seated—Lady Henrietta and Bitty taking up most of the couch, Pepper lounging in an armchair, Lauda perched on the edge of another chair, and Claude barely occupying the corner of a third— Officer Basilier moves to stand directly in front of them. The Duke remains by the fireplace, his expression neutral but attentive.

"You are all here," Officer Basilier begins, her voice clipped and authoritative, "because a man has been assaulted, and the Crown Jewels— are missing. I'll start with an update on the guard— Anthony's— condition. He's stable, but unconscious. The hospital says he may never wake up. If he fails to revive, this will become a murder investigation."

Murmurs rock the room.

"Furthermore," Officer Basilier continues, "the Crown Jewels of Monrovia have been stolen. And each of you had access and opportunity."

"This is outrageous!" Lady Henrietta immediately protests, but Officer Basilier silences her with a raised hand.

"Let me be clear," the officer continues. "The diamond tiara, ruby heart necklace, the diamond ring, and the pearl bracelet disappeared sometime between their final inspection at 7 a.m. and their scheduled public presentation at 11 a.m. When the display was unveiled in the town square, the case was empty. There's been no sign of forced entry on the case itself, which means the jewels were taken before they left the museum."

Through our hidden window, I watch each suspect's reaction. Lady Henrietta rolls her eyes dramatically, while Bitty mirrors her expression with slightly less conviction. Pepper's face remains neutral, but I notice her fingers drumming restlessly on the chair arm. Lauda's eyes widen, and she clutches her folder tighter. Claude dabs his forehead again, looking like he might actually faint.

"Each of you," Officer Basilier continues, pacing slowly in front of them, "was in the museum during this critical time period."

She stops in front of Lady Henrietta and Bitty. "Lady Henrietta and Bitty arrived at 8:30 AM for an 'exclusive preview' of the jewels for Lady Henrietta's social media accounts. You were photographed with the display case."

"Yes, and the jewels still were there when we took our photos," Lady Henrietta says, flipping her hair. "I would hardly pose with an empty case, would I? It would get absolutely no likes."

"We have timestamps on those photos," Bitty adds, pulling out her phone. "I can show you—"

"We've already seen them," Officer Basilier cuts her off.

She moves to stand in front of Lauda. "Dr. Lauda, as curator, you had 24/7 access to the museum and all its exhibits."

Lauda nods, adjusting her glasses. "Yes, but I was in my office all morning preparing for the opening. It's my first major exhibition since completing my PhD, and there were last-minute details to finalize. I only left to check on the final preparations in the main hall."

"Did you see the jewels during this check?" Officer Basilier asks.

"Not directly," Lauda admits. "They were already covered for transport by that point. Claude had just finished cleaning them."

Officer Basilier pivots to Claude, who visibly shrinks under her gaze. "Claude, you were the last person confirmed to have seen the jewels before they disappeared. You cleaned them at 9:15 AM, correct?"

Claude nods, dabbing his forehead again. "Y-yes, that's correct. It's my duty as Royal Jeweler to ensure they're pristine, especially before public display."

"And then what did you do?" Officer Basilier presses.

"I-I covered the display case with the velvet cloth," Claude explains, his voice trembling. "Then I went to get a cup of coffee at *Le Petite Scone*. I was g-gone perhaps fifteen minutes. When I returned, the case was still covered, exactly as I'd left it."

"And you didn't look under the cover?" Officer Basilier's tone is incredulous.

"N-no," Claude admits, looking miserable. "I had no reason to suspect... they were secure in a locked case and Anthony was standing guard at the front entrance of the museum the entire time. I wheeled them out at 10:45 a.m. for the 11 a.m. presentation. There were no guests in the museum at that time. I never imagined..."

Officer Basilier makes a note in her small notebook, then turns to Pepper. "And you, Miss. Our external security cameras caught you entering the museum through a staff entrance at 9:40 a.m. Care to explain what you were doing sneaking into a secure building?"

Pepper sits up straighter, her defiance melting into something more defensive. "I wasn't 'sneaking' anywhere. The door was propped open by a cleaning cart."

"That doesn't explain why you entered," Officer Basilier points out.

Pepper sighs dramatically. "Fine. I was putting up flyers in the entryway. Flyers explaining that monarchy is an outdated system and displaying these jewels glorifies wealth inequality. I was hoping when people went into the museum, they'd see all the flyers and join our cause."

The Duke, who has been silent until now, chuckles softly. "Flyers against the Royal family? I hope if you put my picture on them you chose my good side..."

The tension in the room breaks slightly as even Officer Basilier's mouth twitches.

Pepper looks surprised for a moment, then offers a grudging smile. "I went with a front-facing shot from last year's charity marathon. You looked appropriately sweaty and common, just like everybody else. Because you're not actually special."

"Excellent choice," the Duke nods, apparently unoffended. "Although I'd like to think when I sweat, I'm just *glistening*."

Officer Basilier clears her throat, clearly annoyed by this tangent. "So you claim you only went as far as the entryway to distribute unauthorized flyers?"

"Yes," Pepper confirms. "I didn't even know the jewels were there. I was focused on the opening reception area, where people would actually see my message."

"Convenient," Officer Basilier notes, making another entry in her notebook.

She turns back to Lauda. "As curator, where were *you* when Claude returned with his coffee?"

Lauda straightens. "In my office, as I mentioned. I saw Claude briefly when he was cleaning the Crown Jewels around 9:15, but I didn't see him return. My office is on the second floor, overlooking the garden, not the main exhibition hall."

"Did you notice anything unusual that morning? Any visitors who shouldn't have been there? Any strange noises?" Officer Basilier presses.

Lauda shakes her head. "Nothing out of the ordinary. There was the usual pre-opening bustle— cleaning staff, security doing their rounds— but they all left before the time-window you're describing. Claude was with the jewels. Lady Henrietta and her friend arrived for their photos, but that was scheduled."

"This is absurd!" Lady Henrietta interjects, her voice rising. "I am a member of the Royal Family. Those jewels are part of my heritage. Why would I steal what's already mine?"

"They're not yours," the Duke corrects gently. "They belong to the crown, which is why we were displaying them in the museum— so all citizens could appreciate their historical significance."

"Whatever," Lady Henrietta waves dismissively. "The point is, I didn't take them. Bitty and I were there for exactly twelve minutes. We took the photos and left for brunch at *Le Petite Scone*."

"The same café where Claude went for coffee," Officer Basilier notes, raising an eyebrow.

"It's the only decent café in the village," Bitty points out. "Everyone goes there!"

"Were the jewels in the case when you photographed them?" Officer Basilier asks Lady Henrietta directly.

"Of course they were!" Lady Henrietta pulls out her phone, scrolling through photos. "See? There I am with the tiara right behind me. And here's one with the ruby necklace. They were definitely there."

From our hiding spot, I can see Officer Basilier studying the photos carefully. "And you didn't touch the case? Open it? Move it in any way?"

"Absolutely not," Lady Henrietta sniffs. "Claude was hovering like a nervous hen the whole time. He wouldn't let me within three feet of the actual case."

Claude nods frantically. "It's true. I was most particular about the distance. The oils from human skin can damage the metals and stones."

Officer Basilier turns to face all of them, her expression hard. "Someone in this room knows what happened to those jewels. They didn't just vanish into thin air. Until they're recovered, you are all persons of interest in this investigation."

"You can't possibly think that I—" Lady Henrietta begins.

"I don't care who you are or who you're related to," Officer Basilier cuts her off. "The law applies equally to everyone in Monrovia. None of you are to leave town until this matter is resolved. I will be conducting individual interviews starting tomorrow morning." She turns to the Duke. "Your Grace, I appreciate your cooperation in this matter."

The Duke nods solemnly. "Of course, Officer Basilier. The Crown Jewels aren't just valuable— they're an important part of our national heritage. I want them recovered as much as you do."

"All of you are free to go for now," Officer Basilier announces to the group. "But don't leave town. I'm going to get to the bottom of this— one way or another."

As the suspects begin to rise, their expressions capturing the tone of a difficult day. Lady Henrietta looks outraged, and Bitty mimics her, the two of them stomping from the room in a huff. Claude dabs at his forehead with a handkerchief, hands shaking as he runs from the room. Pepper approaches Officer Basilier and says, "I appreciate you're considering even the Royal suspects," loud enough that Lady Henrietta can hear from the hallway. Meanwhile, Lauda clutches her folder like a shield, gliding out of the room as if she'd rather be anywhere else.

I back away from the one-way mirror, glancing at Maggie as I process everything I've just witnessed. Five people, five different stories, and somewhere in that tangle of alibis and explanations lies the truth about the missing Crown Jewels. Joe senses my shift in mood and presses his warm bulk against my leg, his amber eyes looking up at me with canine curiosity. He always knows when I'm working through a puzzle.

"Well," Maggie whispers, stepping back from the mirror herself, "that was illuminating."

We start making our way back through the passage, Joe leading the way as if he's done this a hundred times. The soft lights illuminate our path, and I find myself already mentally sorting through the suspects and their stories.

"Did you notice how Claude kept wiping his forehead?" I ask. "The man looked like he was about to pass out from guilt."

"Or anxiety," Maggie points out. "He's responsible for the Royal jewels. If they were stolen on his watch, his career is over."

I nod, scratching Joe behind the ears as I think. "And Pepper was awfully quick with that story about putting up flyers. Convenient that she only went to the entryway and nowhere near the jewels."

"True," Maggie says, "but Lady Henrietta and Bitty had the most obvious opportunity. They were literally posing for photos next to the jewels right before they disappeared."

"The timing is the key," I say as we navigate the narrow corridor. "The jewels were there when Claude cleaned them at 9:15. Lady Henrietta's photos show them still there at 9:35. But by the time Claude brought them out to the square at 11:00, they were gone."

"So our window is between 9:35a.m. and 11:00 a.m.," Maggie confirms. "About an hour and twenty-five minutes when someone managed to open a locked display case, remove three priceless jewels, and vanish without a trace."

We reach the end of the passage, and Maggie pushes on the back of the bookcase. It swings open silently, revealing the cozy sitting room exactly as we left it. Joe trots out first, shaking himself as if to rid his golden coat of cobwebs collected from the secret corridor. I step out after him, blinking in the brighter light of the sitting room. It feels strange to be back in the normal world after our clandestine observation session.

Maggie follows, carefully closing the bookcase behind us. She presses the spine of the red book back into place, and there's a soft click as the mechanism locks.

"I'm glad the Duke kept these passages," she says with a small smile. "They come in handy."

"That they do," a voice says from the doorway. Jack— the Duke— is standing there, grinning from ear to ear as if he's caught us in a game of tag.

Joe runs over to him and Maggie and I exchange a glance. I lean over to her, muttering, "I guess you're not the only one who knows about the secret passages."

CHAPTER

Five

AFTER CATCHING us at the exit to the secret passageway, the Duke invites us into one of the castle's many sitting rooms for tea. The room's elegant cream walls and ornate moldings make me feel like I've wandered onto a movie set, but the steaming cup of Earl Grey in front of me is real enough. Joe lies on a velvet pillow beside me, working his way through a plate of butter cookies that Maggie slipped him when she thought no one was looking. The Duke sits across from us, his concerned expression juxtapose against the room's refined atmosphere.

"I guess I should have known you three would investigate," Jack smiles, lifting a delicate porcelain teapot to refill our cups. His hands are steady, but I notice the slight furrow between his brows. "Though I must say, Joe seems more interested in the refreshments than detective work."

Joe looks up at the mention of his name, cookie crumbs decorating his golden muzzle.

"He multitasks," I explain. "Right now he's gathering energy for later crime-solving activities."

The Duke's lips twitch upward, but the worry doesn't leave his eyes. "I don't suppose I can talk you out of it?"

Maggie and I exchange glances. There's no need for words — we've already made up our minds. The jewels need to be found, and frankly, I don't trust Officer Basilier to handle this with the care it deserves.

The Duke reads our expressions and sighs deeply. He sets his teacup down with a gentle clink against the saucer. "I thought as much."

"Your Grace," Maggie begins, but he raises a hand.

"Jack, please. At least when it's just us." His voice softens. "We're all friends, more than co-workers, aren't we? After all that's happened?"

Friends. The word makes me deflate a little. Maybe the Duke *doesn't* see me as a romantic interest, and our dinner this weekend is simply a friendly one.

"And truth be told, I could actually use your help," Jack continues. "Though I hate to put any of you in potential danger."

I lean forward slightly. "Is that what you think? That whoever took the jewels is dangerous?"

Jack runs a hand through his salt-and-pepper hair, mussing it slightly in a way that makes him look less like a Duke and more like an ordinary worried man. "I don't know. But I *do* know that I don't trust Officer Basilier to handle this properly."

"Because of what happened with Rodrigo?" Maggie asks quietly.

The name hangs in the air between us. Rodrigo—the gossip magazine owner who was found dead just weeks ago. Maggie and I solved the case after Officer Basilier accused the Duke.

Jack nods grimly. "She was more interested in pointing fingers than finding actual evidence. Made a spectacle of the whole tragedy." He looks directly at me. "I want justice for the guard, Anthony, and I hope he wakes up. I've sent for the finest doctors in Monrovia to come to Atwood Hospital and assist in his recovery. But other than that, there's nothing I can do for him. I must shift my focus to finding out who did this. That's my concern now. The jewels themselves are valuable, yes, but I'm not losing sleep over their monetary worth. It's something more."

"What?" I ask, watching him carefully.

He takes a deep breath. "The future of Atwood. The museum was meant to be a turning point for this town." His voice turns passionate, his hands gesturing as he speaks. "I invested a significant portion of the town's treasury in restoring that monastery, transforming it into something that could support the local economy for generations."

"The jewels were the main attraction," Maggie says.

"Exactly," Jack confirms, running his finger along the rim of his teacup. "Without them, attendance will drop dramatically. The museum might have to close, and if that happens..." He doesn't finish the sentence, but he doesn't have to.

"The town suffers," Maggie completes his thought, her face serious. "Shops, restaurants, local artisans—everyone who was counting on tourist traffic."

I feel Joe nudge my hand with his nose, sensing my shifting mood. This isn't just about missing gems. It's about people's livelihoods.

"I've decided to continue moving forward with the museum's grand opening even without the Crown Jewels," Jack adds, looking forlorn. "I'm hoping we can salvage the event and still bring awareness to the new museum attraction in Atwood. But I fear— without the crown jewels— our efforts will be made in vain."

"We want to help," I say firmly. "We're already involved, whether we like it or not. Maggie, Joe, and I can solve this." At the mention of his name, Joe gives a soft "*woof*" that sounds like agreement.

"And Atwood is our home," Maggie adds. "If there's something we can do to help the village, we want to do it."

Jack looks between us, his expression unreadable for a moment. Then something in his face shifts, a decision made. "Then I suppose we'd better make it official."

"Does that mean we have your blessing to investigate?" I ask.

"It would mean a lot more than just my blessing," Jack says, straightening in his chair. "If you're serious about this, perhaps it would help if I gave you an official title." A playful glint appears in his eye, momentarily displacing the worry. "Royal Investigators?"

Maggie nearly spits out her tea. "Are you serious?"

"Perfectly serious," Jack confirms. "If you're going to look into this, you might as well have some authority behind you. Officer Basilier won't like it, but she'll have to acknowledge Royal prerogative."

The idea of having an actual title makes me feel strangely giddy, like a kid being handed a toy badge. Except this badge would carry real weight. "Royal Investigator Rebecca Orange," I try out the words. "It has a nice ring to it."

"Royal Investigator Maggie Lefevere doesn't sound too shabby either," Maggie adds with a grin.

"What about Joe? Is he an honorary investigator?" I ask, glancing down at my furry companion.

Jack's smile widens. "With those observational skills? Absolutely. I think he's already spotted that I've hidden another cookie in my pocket." As if to prove his point, Joe shifts his attention to the Duke, his tail thumping hopefully against the floor.

The Duke laughs and produces the promised treat from his pocket, holding it out for Joe to take gently from his fingers.

"Maggie, can you draw up some paperwork? And perhaps have a couple of badges made?" Jack asks, turning his attention back to business.

"Of course, Your Grace—Jack," Maggie quickly corrects herself. "I can have them ready by tomorrow morning."

"Excellent." He nods, satisfied. "That should give you three enough official standing to ask questions without Officer Basilier interfering too much. Though I suspect she'll find ways to make her displeasure known."

"I can handle Officer Basilier," I say with more confidence than I actually feel. The truth is, the woman intimidates me a little, but I'm not about to admit that.

Jack's expression turns serious again. "Just be careful, all of you. We don't know who took those jewels or why. The person behind all of this has already shown they're willing to harm others in their pursuit of treasure."

His concern seems genuine, warming me from the inside in a way that has nothing to do with the tea. "We'll be careful," I promise.

Maggie stands up, gathering her tablet. "I should get started on that paperwork. And I'll need to coordinate with the jeweler's staff for statements." Always efficient, she's already mentally ten steps ahead.

"I'll meet you in the press office," Jack offers, standing as well.

As Maggie heads toward the door, Jack pauses beside my chair. I begin to rise, but he gently touches my shoulder. "Rebecca, a moment?"

Joe, sensing something important, sits up straighter at my feet, his eyes moving between Jack and me.

"This doesn't change our plans for Saturday, does it?" Jack asks quietly, referring to the dinner he'd invited me to last week. "I've been looking forward to showing you the village when it's not overrun with tourists or, well, crime scenes."

I feel a flutter in my stomach that has nothing to do with detective work. "It doesn't change a thing," I assure him. "I've been looking forward to it too."

Relief crosses his face, and then, with a formality that

seems both out of place and perfectly right, he takes my hand and brushes his lips lightly across my knuckles. "Until then, Royal Investigator."

The touch sends an unexpected tingle up my arm, and I'm momentarily too surprised to respond. Before I can find my voice, he straightens and follows Maggie toward the door. Joe looks up at me with what I swear is a knowing expression, his tail wagging slowly.

"Oh, hush," I tell him, feeling my cheeks warm. "It's just dinner."

Joe makes a snuffling sound that communicates he's not buying my story.

"And a case," I add, my mind already shifting back to the missing jewels. "We've got work to do, partner."

Joe stands at attention, all business now that the cookies are gone. Together, we exit the room, the weight of our new responsibility settling on my shoulders. *Royal Investigators.* It sounds impressive, but titles don't solve crimes.

Good thing I didn't come to Monrovia for the titles.

———

Later, the setting sun casts long shadows across the Royal Menagerie as I make my quick evening rounds. The enclosures are state-of-the-art, nestled within the castle's east wing where modern glass and steel blend seamlessly with centuries-old stone. Joe trots beside me, his massive frame dwarfing the pathway between habitats as he keeps a watchful eye on the exotic birds that always grab his attention.

"Sorry, guys. Quick dinner tonight," I tell the birds as I measure out their food. Their spotted coats gleam in the fading light as they pace eagerly, waiting for me to step back from their feeding station. Behind them, two African cranes watch me with their intense golden eyes. Ace, the castle hawk, flaps his wings at me.

Twenty minutes later, Joe and I are back inside my apartment in the castle staff wing. The small space is warm and inviting, with french doors that open to a garden space that's all ours.

Joe settles himself on the thick rug in front of the fireplace while I cross my desk. The wall above it displays a simple corkboard—a relic from previous cases I've helped solve in my time here. Without hesitation, I take the board down and prop it against the edge of my desk. From the drawer, I pull out a package of index cards, a handful of colored pins, and a black marker. Joe watches me with quiet interest, his head tilted slightly to one side.

"Five suspects," I tell him, uncapping the marker. "Let's lay them out."

I write each name in clear, block letters:

LADY HENRIETTA
BITTY (LADY-IN-WAITING)
CLAUDE (ROYAL JEWELER)
LAUDA (MUSEUM CURATOR)
PEPPER (PROTESTOR)

Each card gets pinned to the corkboard, forming a neat row. I step back, studying them while absently running my fingers through Joe's thick fur as he moves to stand beside me.

"What do you think, buddy? Who had the means, motive, and opportunity?"

Joe makes a low sound in his throat, his eyes fixed on the board as if he understands exactly what we're doing. And maybe he does, in his way. He's been my partner through tougher challenges than this.

I add a card in the center with "CROWN JEWELS" written on it, then draw lines connecting it to each suspect. A blank card goes beneath each name, waiting for notes on their potential motives.

I know the truth is here, and I'm going to find it, I think, tapping the marker against my palm as I study the names. Just because I'm not Royal doesn't mean I can't contribute to this country. And to Jack.

My gaze drifts to the window, where the lights of Atwood village twinkle in the gathering darkness. In just a few months, this place has become more than just a job location—it's become somewhere I care about deeply. The people here have welcomed me, made me feel valued for my expertise rather than my pedigree.

"This isn't about impressing a Duke or earning a fancy title," I tell Joe softly. "It's about helping these people."

Joe presses his warm side against my leg in silent support.

I turn back to the corkboard with renewed determination. There's a truth to uncover, and I intend to find it—not for recognition or reward, but because Monrovia deserves nothing less. I may not have royal blood flowing through my veins, but that doesn't make this country any less worth fighting for.

"Time to get to work," I say, picking up my notebook. "We've got a mystery to solve."

CHAPTER
Six

THE NEXT MORNING, light streams through the windows of *Cafe de Flore*, catching on the vases of fresh flowers that dot every table. I'm still getting used to the idea that this quaint village cafe, with its books stacked on wooden shelves and floral-inspired drinks, is now part of my regular life. Joe sits at my feet, his massive frame tucked neatly under our table as Maggie spreads papers between our coffee cups and lays out our plan for the day.

"Looks like you're not just the castle animal trainer anymore! We're Royal Investigators," she says, emphasizing the word *royal*. "If we're going to do this, we've got to be professionals about it."

I take a sip of my own rose-infused coffee, which tastes exactly like it sounds—floral, sweet, and somehow not at all like drinking perfume.

"Do professionals eat omeletes while they work?" I ask.

Right on time, Jocelyn approaches with our food. "I hope they do," she winks at me, making it clear she overhead my question. She sets down plates loaded with flaky pastries, fresh fruit, and what smells like the best quiche I've encountered since crossing the Atlantic. "One sunrise breakfast plate, one flower garden omelet, and one doggy breakfast bowl." She bends down to place a specially prepared dish in front of Joe, who responds with his most dignified woof of appreciation. Jocelyn wipes her hands on her apron, adding, "Your meals are on us today."

"No, we can't possibly let you—" Maggie starts to say, but Jocelyn waves a hand at her, cutting her off.

"It's my pleasure," Jocelyn leans in conspiratorially, whispering, "we're all counting on you to solve this mystery and save our museum exhibition. It means so much to the village."

As she walks away, I turn to Maggie with raised eyebrows. "Word travels fast around here."

Maggie shrugs, already cutting into her colorful omelet studded with edible flowers. "Small town, big castle, bigger gossip. We might as well use it to our advantage. People are more likely to talk if they know you're officially on the case." Maggie's eyes light up. "That reminds me!" She reaches into her bag and pulls out a small leather case. "I had this made for you yesterday. The Duke approved it this morning."

She hands it to me, and I flip it open to reveal a gold badge—an actual, official-looking badge with the Royal Crest of Monrovia and the words "Royal Investigator" engraved beneath it. My name is there too, professionally etched into the metal.

"This looks... very real," I say, running my finger over the raised lettering.

"It is real!" Maggie beams. "I got myself one too, so we match."

I tuck the badge into my pocket, surprised by how "right" the gesture feels. I'd never considered becoming a private investigator, but then again, I'd also never imagined living in a castle in a foreign country or having a crush on a Duke. *Life is full of surprises*, I think to myself.

"Alright," I say to Maggie, all business. "Who should we interview today?"

"I called the museum to check that Lauda would be there, and they said she's working until later tonight. Might be worth stopping by to talk to her."

I nod, agreeing. "While we're there we should also start with the scene of the crime. See the empty display, get a feel for where the jewels were before they disappeared."

"Good thinking," Maggie says. "We should bring something for Lauda to soften her up a bit. A peace offering of sorts. She's been through a lot of questioning already."

I glance toward the cafe's display counter, where an array of colorful macarons sits behind glass. "How about a few of those? They look amazing."

"Perfect. The rose-flavored ones are their specialty—matches the whole floral theme."

Fifteen minutes later, we're walking down the cobblestone street toward the museum, a small box containing a few delicate rose macarons tucked safely in Maggie's bag. Joe trots happily alongside us, and my new badge burns a hole in my pocket. I'm not sure what we'll find, but for the first time since the theft was discovered, I feel like we might actually have a chance of solving this mystery.

———

Lauda's office is as stunning as the rest of the monastery-turned-museum, its ancient stone walls untouched by the recent renovation. An expansive window hovers over her desk, which is made of modern metal and feels out of place in the ancient setting. Lauda taps her fingers next to her keyboard, peering over at us from her computer.

"Thanks for meeting with us," I say, eager to befriend the woman who knows the most about the museum. "We know you've been through plenty of questioning already."

"It never ends," Lauda agrees. "All I wanted was a normal job. A good experience— to start my career…"

Joe— sensing his cue— sits perfectly and offers a paw to comfort her, placing it on her knee. His dignified posture is somewhat undermined by his wagging tail.

Lauda relaxes slightly but looks down at his paw like he's an alien creature. "I'm sorry, it's just—with everything that's happened, I'm a bit on edge. Can you—"

"No problem," I say, whistling at Joe so he returns to my side.

I can see the skepticism in Lauda's eyes, so I pull out my shiny new badge. "The Duke has asked us to look into the theft. Officially."

"Oh!" Lauda's eyebrows rise. "I didn't realize he was bringing in outside help. The police have already been through everything several times."

"Sometimes fresh eyes notice things others might miss."

Maggie reaches into her bag. "We brought you something from *Cafe de Flore*. Just a small gesture—we know this must be incredibly stressful for you."

She holds out the little box containing the rose macarons. Lauda accepts it with a surprised smile that quickly turns apologetic.

"That's very kind. Thank you. I'm actually on a diet, but..." She opens the box and looks at the delicate pink confection. "Maybe just a bite won't hurt."

She takes a small, careful bite, closes her eyes briefly, then quickly closes the box again. She savors the taste, which tells me her diet must be strict. "Mmm. I'll save the rest for later. It's delicious."

"You must be under enormous pressure right now," I say sympathetically.

Lauda's professional composure cracks just slightly. "You have no idea. This position... it was like winning the lottery." She glances around to make sure no visitors are within earshot before continuing. "Do you know how many people applied for this curator position? Seventy-three. I spent six years getting my PhD in Monrovian History and Art, and the academic job market here is absolutely brutal." She pushes her glasses up her nose. "When I got this position, my dissertation advisor actually cried with relief. She'd been worried I'd end up waiting tables with a doctorate. Becoming an academic today is more like trying to be a celebrity. If you want any career at all you have to be visible, have press interviews, publish in prestigious journals. I'm so lucky I even got *this* position as a curator— my real dream is to be a professor, but I'm grateful to have ended up anywhere."

"And then *this* happens on your opening day," I say sympathetically.

"Exactly." Lauda's voice tightens. She looks down at her tablet, fingers gripping it so hard her knuckles whiten. "I keep running through that morning over and over in my head, trying to figure out what I missed."

Joe whines quietly, sensing her distress. I place a calming hand on his head.

"Did anything strange happen that morning?"

"Nothing," Lauda assures me. "The jewels were there when I checked on them before the big reveal. I walked past them a few times after that but didn't see them directly because they were covered. Claude insisted on keeping them covered in a piece of cloth at all times to block the light. He said the exposure could wash them out, making the colors less vibrant."

I nod thoughtfully. "We'd like to speak with Claude, the Royal Jeweler. Is here today?"

"No. After the theft he was..." she says, her tone carefully neutral. "... well, inconsolable is putting it mildly. He's staying at the castle, in one of the guest rooms across from Lady Henrietta's suite."

"And what about the murder weapon?" I ask. "We heard Officer Basilier say Anthony was bludgeoned over the head with a statue of some kind that was kept here in the museum?"

Lauda nods. "Yes, it was a Monrovian statue of a woman holding a heart in her hands. It's been cleaned of blood and returned to its place in the bronze age exhibit. Thankfully, it survived the attack."

So much for Anthony, I think. *But yes, glad the statue survived.*

"Is it possible for us to see where the jewels were displayed?" I ask.

Lauda hesitates. "It's cordoned off with police tape. They've processed the scene, but asked us not to disturb anything."

"We'll be very careful," I promise. "Joe has an excellent nose—he might pick up something the human investigators missed."

"A scent? After all this time?" Lauda sounds skeptical.

I smile. "You'd be surprised what he can detect. At the Safari Park, he once tracked a missing monkey through three miles of park grounds after it escaped."

This seems to impress her, though hesitation still lingers in her expression. "I suppose it's alright. The Duke *did* authorize your investigation, after all." She tucks her tablet under her arm. "Follow me."

As we walk through the main exhibition hall, I take in the other displays. Cultural artifacts, historical documents, and various royal heirlooms fill the elegant cases, each with detailed descriptions and historical context.

"It's a beautiful exhibition," I tell Lauda sincerely. "You've done an amazing job with the presentation."

Her posture straightens slightly at the praise. "Thank you. We've tried to make Monrovian history accessible to everyone. That was the Duke's vision—to bring these treasures out of storage and share them with the people."

We turn down a corridor where the stone walls give way

to a smaller, more intimate gallery. Small statues line the displays.

"Is that—" Maggie starts to ask, pointing at a statue of a woman holding a heart in her hands.

"The weapon, yes," Lauda nods. "It's ironic— the sculpture is of the late Queen Eleanora. The same one who named the Crown Jewels. A merchant named Sir Edmund Blackwell fell in love with her in the 18th century. Because he wasn't royal, they couldn't marry—"

"Maggie told me the story about the jewels," I say, drawn to the statue of the Queen. Her arms are outstretched, her eyes filled with longing. As I look at the colors within, I can't help but think about Jack and me. *Would a romance ever work between us?* I'm a commoner and Jack is Royalty. Still, a girl can dream.

"And now they're gone," Maggie says quietly.

Lauda's expression tightens. "Yes. Through here."

She leads us to a doorway blocked by yellow police tape. Beyond it, I can see a small gallery with a single display case in the center—empty now, with its glass top open like a mouth frozen mid-scream.

"This is it," Lauda says. "The Crown Jewel Gallery."

"May we?" I gesture toward the tape.

After a moment's hesitation, Lauda nods. "Just... please be careful. And technically, I shouldn't let the dog in."

I glance down at Joe, who looks up at me with a soft expression.

"Joe is more well-behaved than most people," I assure her. "He won't disturb anything."

Lauda nods reluctantly. "Alright. I need to check on another gallery, but I'll be back in a few minutes. Please don't touch anything."

Lauda exits, and we step under the police tape, Joe padding quietly behind us. The Crown Jewel Gallery feels like a tomb. The room itself isn't large—maybe twenty feet square

—but the vaulted ceiling and stone walls make our footsteps echo slightly. Sunlight filters through a single stained glass window, illuminating dust particles that dance in the beam of colored light. At the center of it all stands the empty display case, its lid propped open, the velvet lining inside still bearing the gentle impressions where the Crown Jewels once rested.

"It's eerie," Maggie whispers, her voice still somehow loud in the silence. "Like a grave that's been robbed."

"In a way, it is," I reply, approaching the display case carefully. "These jewels weren't just valuable objects—they were someone's legacy."

I circle the display, taking in every detail. The case itself is modern despite its antique appearance.

"Whoever took the jewels had to have had access to a key to unlock the case," I think outloud. "Unless Claude left it unlocked on accident. Or he was working with someone."

Joe follows close behind me as I continue my circuit around the case. His nose works overtime, taking in scents that I can only imagine. I've worked with him long enough to read his body language—right now, he's interested but not alerting to anything specific.

I peer closer at the velvet. The cushioned fabric is cut into the shape of a tiara, necklace, ring, and bracelet. "No signs of tearing or forced removal. The jewels were lifted out with care."

Joe sniffs more intently at the base of the display, his tail swishing back and forth in that particular way he has when he's found something interesting.

"What is it, boy?" I ask, watching him circle the pedestal. His nose moves methodically across the floor, following some invisible trail that only he can detect.

I begin my own careful examination of the floor surrounding the display case. The ancient stone floor of the monastery has been preserved, its uneven surface creating countless tiny shadows and crevices where small items might hide from human eyes.

While Joe continues his investigation, I pull a small flashlight from my pocket—a habit from my days working with nocturnal animals—and shine it at a low angle across the floor, using the light to create longer shadows that might reveal what Joe has sensed.

"Good thinking," Maggie says, stepping back to give me room to work.

The beam catches something in a small gap between two stones, about a foot from the display case. I almost miss it—a tiny object nestled in the ancient mortar.

"There's something there," I say, pointing to the spot. I'm about to reach for it when I remember Lauda's warning about not touching anything. Technically, she only asked *me* not to touch anything. Joe is a free agent.

"Joe, retrieve," I command, pointing to the spot.

Joe's training kicks in immediately. With a delicacy that always amazes people who don't understand working dogs, he approaches the exact spot I've indicated. His massive head lowers, and with surgical precision, he gently takes whatever it is between his front teeth. Then he returns to me, sitting perfectly at attention, waiting for me to accept what he's found.

"Good boy," I praise, holding out my hand.

Joe deposits the tiny object in my palm, and I bring it closer to examine. Maggie leans in beside me.

"Is that... a seed?" she asks.

I turn it over carefully with my fingertip. "It's a sunflower seed. Still in its shell."

"What's a sunflower seed doing here?"

I frown, considering. "It's out of place in a museum, especially one this meticulously maintained."

"You think it fell from our thief?" Maggie asks.

"Possibly." I stand up, still holding the seed. "Joe, search. More of these."

Joe understands the command, his nose returning to the floor as he quarters the room systematically. After a thorough search, he returns to me without finding any additional seeds.

"Just the one, then," I murmur.

Maggie looks thoughtful. "Should we bag it as evidence?"

I nod, pulling a small plastic bag from my pocket—another holdover from my animal work, where collecting samples is routine. I carefully place the seed inside and seal it.

"I don't want to jump to conclusions," I say, "It could be nothing. But it could be… *something.*"

I walk back to the display case, studying it with fresh eyes. "The bigger question is how they got the jewels out of the museum. The tiara alone would be difficult to conceal, let alone all the pieces together. I'm surprised they didn't put in security cameras."

"The renovation was so rushed," Maggie agrees. "And they wanted to maintain the monastery's original charm. Honestly, I think they believed the guard would be enough."

Having thoroughly searched the scene of the crime, we duck back under the police tape and exit the Crown Jewel Gallery, heading toward the museum's exit. I can't help but wonder about the logistics of the theft. *How did the thief get out with the jewels, without being seen?*

"What's bothering me," I whisper to Maggie as we walk, "is not just how someone got the jewels out of the museum, but why. These aren't items you can easily sell on the black market without getting caught. What's the motivation if not monetary gain?"

"Maybe it's not about selling them," Maggie suggests. "Maybe it's about possessing them. Or preventing the museum from displaying them."

That thought sticks with me as we exit the cordoned area.

I grip the small bag containing the sunflower seed in my pocket. It's not much to go on, but it's a start.

CHAPTER
Seven

THE THICK, wooden door of the Royal Heritage Museum closes behind us with a heavy thud that echoes through the stone courtyard. After examining the empty display cases where the crown jewels should be, I'm ready for fresh air and a moment to clear my head. Joe's massive paws click-clack on the cobblestones beside me, his golden coat catching the afternoon sun as Maggie checks something on her tablet. We've barely made it ten steps when I spot trouble brewing just outside the museum gates.

Pepper.

"She's still at it," Maggie laughs, nodding toward Pepper, who's pacing outside the museum with a sign. "The woman won't give up!"

"Looks like it," I say, watching as Officer Basilier scribbles furiously on a citation pad. "And it seems like the local police aren't too thrilled with her anarchist manifesto."

Officer Basilier's uniform is, as I've come to expect from her, pressed to perfection. Even from this distance, I can see the muscles in her forearms flex as she writes the ticket. I almost feel bad for Pepper, because I know what it's like to cross paths with the Officer.

Joe lets out a small whine, sensing the tension ahead. I give his leash a gentle tug, keeping him close as we approach.

"—completely ridiculous!" Pepper's voice carries across the courtyard. "I've been protesting here all week! You can't just suddenly decide my permit isn't valid!"

Officer Basilier doesn't even look up from her citation pad. "Your permit expired yesterday at midnight. It's not my job to remind you to renew it."

"But the application is still pending! I submitted it three days ago!"

"Then you should have waited for approval before continuing your protest." Officer Basilier tears the ticket off her pad with a decisive rip and holds it out. "One hundred and fifty euros. Payable within thirty days."

Pepper snatches the ticket, her fishnet-covered arms trembling with rage. "This is exactly what I'm protesting! The arbitrary enforcement of rules to silence dissent!"

"Feel free to note that in your appeal." Officer Basilier finally looks up, her gaze immediately landing on us. Her eyes narrow, focusing particularly on Joe. "Is that animal permitted on these grounds?"

Before I can answer, Joe's tail starts wagging with hurricane force. He's never met a human he didn't immediately love, regardless of how unpleasant they might be. This is why, despite his imposing 250-pound frame, he fails spectacularly as a guard dog.

"He's a working dog."

Officer Basilier's lips press into a thin line.

Maggie steps forward, taking out her badge. She holds out the official-looking regalia, which features the royal crest of Monrovia. "We're here on Royal business regarding the missing crown jewels."

"Under whose authority?"

Maggie doesn't miss a beat, almost joyful at the opportunity to bother Officer Basilier. "The Duke of Atwood himself, Officer. He's personally requested our assistance in the investigation." I follow suit, pulling out my own newly issued credentials and flashing them at Officer Basilier, unable to keep a smile from crossing my face.

"The Monrovian Police have jurisdiction here, not the Duke's household staff."

I can feel my hackles rising. "We're not interfering with your investigation. We're conducting our own internal inquiry at the request of the Duke. The Crown Jewels are family property."

"Jewels that are now evidence in a theft case, and attempted murder," Officer Basilier counters. She steps closer, and despite being at least six inches shorter than me, somehow manages to make me feel like I'm being towered over. "Let me make something very clear, Ms. Orange. The last time the Royal Family tried to handle a criminal matter internally, a murderer nearly escaped justice."

And you almost blamed everything on the Duke! I think, biting my tongue. Without Maggie and me, the wrong person would have been sent to prison.

"That was a completely different situation," Maggie says diplomatically. "And the police were brought in immediately—"

"And *your* interference slowed our progress," Officer Basilier interrupts. "I don't care who you work for or what fancy title they've given you. This is *my* investigation, and I won't have castle staff playing detective and muddying the waters."

Joe chooses this moment to let out a friendly "woof" and strain forward on his leash, clearly interpreting Officer Basilier's intensity as an invitation to become best friends. I tighten my grip.

"Joe, stay," I command, but it's too late. All 250 pounds of pure Tibetan Mastiff enthusiasm lunges forward, dragging me a step closer to Officer Basilier. I manage to halt his progress, but not before he's close enough for his massive head to be at perfect petting height.

Officer Basilier takes a step back, her hand instinctively moving to rest on her baton.

"He's friendly," I say quickly. "Just... overly friendly. Joe, sit."

Joe plops his enormous rear end onto the cobblestones, looking up at Officer Basilier with what I can only describe as adoration in his eyes. His tail sweeps back and forth across the ground, creating a small dust cloud.

"Keep that animal under control," Officer Basilier says, but I can't help but notice the admiration in her voice. "Even if he is quite… beautiful," she adds begrudgingly, stopping to pet his head, despite herself. "And as for your 'internal inquiry,' I suggest you leave the real investigation to professionals."

I've worked with enough alpha personalities in the animal world to recognize when someone's marking their territory. And like with most territorial displays, backing down just invites more aggression.

"We'll be sure to stay out of your way," I say carefully. "But the Duke has asked us to investigate and document the security breach for the royal records. I'm sure we can coordinate our efforts."

"There's nothing to coordinate," Officer Basilier snaps. "The Monrovian Police don't answer to the Duke, despite what he may think. We answer to the people of Monrovia."

Pepper, who's been watching this exchange with undisguised interest, snorts loudly. "Since when? You enforce the monarchy's rules, just like everyone else in this country."

Officer Basilier whirls around. "I've given you your citation. I suggest you take it and go, unless you'd like to add disorderly conduct to your charges."

Pepper raises her hands in mock surrender but doesn't move.

Officer Basilier turns back to us, her eyes like flints. "Let me be perfectly clear. If I find either of you interfering with my investigation—questioning witnesses, collecting evidence, or conducting any activity that could compromise this case—I will arrest you for obstruction of justice."

"We understand completely," Maggie says, her tone professional but edged with steely determination. "We'll be sure to keep the Duke informed of your... concerns."

Officer Basilier holds Maggie's gaze for a long moment, then shifts to me. "Remember what I said, Miss Orange. This isn't castle grounds. Out here, a badge with a royal crest doesn't mean much."

With that parting shot, she turns on her heel and strides away, her back ramrod straight. I watch her go, feeling like I've just had a close encounter with a particularly angry badger.

"Well," I say, once Officer Basilier is out of earshot. "She's always delightful."

"Can I pet him?" Pepper asks, her tough exterior softening as she looks at Joe. "I love dogs. They don't believe in hierarchical power structures either."

I laugh despite myself. "Go ahead. Joe believes everyone was put on this earth specifically to give him belly rubs."

"You're just a big sweetie, aren't you?" Pepper says, scratching under Joe's chin. "Not like your masters at the castle, huh?" Pepper turns her gaze toward Maggie and me. "Why exactly are you two investigating the jewels? It's actually a good thing they're gone, you know."

Her tone shifts so quickly from dog-lover to confrontational activist that it gives me whiplash. I exchange a quick glance with Maggie, who offers a slight nod. Time to see what we can learn.

"The Duke asked us to look into it," I say, watching

Pepper's reaction carefully. "The Crown Jewels are historically significant."

Pepper scoffs, giving Joe one final pat before standing up. Her black and red outfit—classic anarchist colors, I realize—seems at odds with the gentle way she just treated Joe.

"Historically significant?" She rolls her eyes dramatically. "They're symbols of oppression, that's what they are. Some rich guy gave them to his royal girlfriend hundreds of years ago and now everyone acts like they're sacred artifacts."

"They're part of Monrovian heritage," Maggie interjects politely. "Many people feel connected to them."

"People feel connected to what they're *told* to feel connected to," Pepper counters, crossing her arms. "You know what would be better than putting those jewels back in a glass case? Selling them and using the money to help actual Monrovians who are struggling."

I've met enough passionate animal rights activists to recognize true conviction when I see it. Pepper isn't just spouting talking points—she genuinely believes what she's saying.

"Is that why you're protesting?" I ask. "You think the jewels should be sold?"

"I'm protesting the entire concept of monarchy," she says, her voice rising with enthusiasm. "Look, humans lived in tribal, self-governing communities for thousands of years before kings and queens came along claiming divine right to rule." She gestures expansively. "People don't need rulers! We're perfectly capable of organizing ourselves into cooperative communities where decisions are made collectively."

Joe sits up, tilting his head at Pepper's increased animation.

"So no government at all?" I ask, genuinely curious. "How would that work exactly?"

Pepper's face lights up at my question, clearly thrilled to have an audience. "Communities would make decisions together, through consensus. If someone causes harm, they face consequences from the community—maybe they're asked to leave if they can't respect the collective good. We don't need police or prisons or kings."

"And what about people who refuse to participate in this consensus?" I ask. "Or those who take advantage of others?"

"They'd be exiled," Pepper says with a shrug. "The community would protect itself. Natural consequences."

"That sounds a bit like government with fewer steps," I observe, then quickly course-correct. I'm not here to debate political philosophy. "Were you at the museum the morning the jewels went missing? Before the theft was discovered?"

Pepper's passionate expression falters slightly, her eyes darting away from mine for just a split second. "I was outside. Protesting. Like I've been doing all week."

"I'm committed to the cause," Pepper says defensively. "I stayed outside with my sign."

She's lying, I think, remembering that we heard Pepper confess to entering the museum when she was cornered by Officer Basilier in the library.

Joe whines softly, looking up at Pepper with what I can only describe as disappointment. Animals have an uncanny ability to sense dishonesty. They don't understand the words, but they read the conflicting signals our bodies send when we lie.

"You didn't happen to see anyone leaving the museum with, say, a bag that looked incredibly heavy or full?" I try. "Or maybe someone acting suspiciously?"

"No," Pepper says, too quickly. "And I didn't take the jewels, if that's what you're implying. Though honestly, whoever took them did Monrovia a favor."

I tilt my head, mimicking Joe's curious posture. "How so?"

"Think about it," she says, leaning in with renewed intensity. "Those jewels are worth what—ten million euros? More? That money should belong to the people, not locked away in some display case where it does no good for anyone. If I *had* taken them—which I didn't—I would have sold them and distributed the money to community organizations, housing cooperatives, mutual aid networks..."

"That's a pretty strong motive you're laying out there," I observe mildly.

Pepper's eyes widen as she realizes what she's just said. "I *didn't* take them! I'm just saying conceptually, it would be better if they stayed gone. They represent everything wrong with monarchy—obscene wealth hoarded by a few while others struggle."

Joe nudges my hand with his wet nose, his signal that he's getting restless. Or perhaps he's trying to tell me something about Pepper. Sometimes I think he understands these interrogations better than I do.

"The jewels going missing shows how ineffective Government is," Pepper adds.

"And without Government who would maintain infrastructure?" Maggie asks, sounding genuinely interested. "Roads, water systems, power grids?"

"Community work initiatives," Pepper answers promptly. "Everyone contributes a few hours each week to maintaining shared resources. We'd actually be more efficient without bureaucracy slowing everything down."

As Pepper speaks, I can't help but notice how young she seems—early twenties at most. There's an idealism to her vision that hasn't yet been tempered by life's complexities. Part of me admires her passion, even if I find her ideas impractical.

"It sounds like you've given this a lot of thought," I say.

"I have my Master's in Political Science," she says proudly. "This isn't just theory for me—I believe another world is possible."

I nod, reassessing her. Not just a young rebel, then, but an educated idealist. That makes her both more and less suspicious in my book. More, because she has the intellectual framework to justify taking the jewels as a political act. Less, because academic revolutionaries often talk big but hesitate when it comes to actually breaking the law.

"Well, we should let you get back to your protest," I say, tugging gently on Joe's leash. "Unless you've remembered anything else about this morning that might help us?"

Pepper hesitates, and for a moment I think she might actually tell us something useful. But then she shakes her head. "Nope. Nothing to add."

"If you do think of anything," Maggie says, offering Pepper a business card, "please call me at the castle. The Duke would be very grateful for any information."

Pepper takes the card with obvious reluctance, holding it between two fingers as if it might contaminate her. "Sure. But like I said, whoever took those jewels did us all a favor."

Joe gives her one last hopeful look, clearly angling for more belly rubs, but I gently lead him away. "Come on, buddy. Time to head back."

As we walk away from Pepper and back toward Castle Atwood, Maggie waits until we're well out of earshot before speaking.

""Do you believe her?"" Maggie asks quietly.

I consider this as we walk along the cobblestone street leading from the village back to the castle grounds. The afternoon sun casts long shadows from the old stone buildings, and Joe trots happily beside us, oblivious to our concerns.

"I believe she thinks the theft was a good thing," I say carefully. "But that doesn't mean she did it. Unless she plans to use the jewels for something specific. Like funding anarchist causes. She mentioned selling them and distributing the money."

"The tiara alone is worth over ten million euros," Maggie says. "That could fund a lot of revolution."

We walk in silence for a moment, both considering the

implications. As we approach the bridge that leads toward the castle, I can't help wonder if Pepper might be right about one thing: maybe the jewels would be better off staying lost. They've already led to poor Anthony ending up in the hospital. Who else might get hurt over gems someone is willing to kill for?

UPON RETURNING TO THE CASTLE, Maggie, Joe and I grab a to-go lunch from Chef Renauld, who arranges a "grab and go" station for castle staff when the weather cooperates. Her picnic lunches are quickly becoming my favorite perk of castle life. The wicker basket swings from my hand as we make our way across the immaculate grounds toward the menagerie. The spring air carries the scent of freshly cut grass and something sweet from the kitchen gardens. Joe trots ahead, occasionally stopping to look back as if to ask why we're walking so slowly when there's lunch to be eaten.

"I swear Chef Renauld outdid herself today," Maggie says, nodding toward the basket. "She made this basket especially for us and nearly slapped my hand when I tried to peek inside. Said it was a special recipe for *'les détectives.'*"

I laugh. "She thinks we're *actual* detectives rather than a household manager and an animal expert playing at solving crimes?"

"Oh, absolutely. She's so proud we've been made Royal Investigators. And she's extremely invested in our success." Maggie adjusts her sunglasses against the bright midday light. "I think she likes the drama of it all."

"Well, I'm just glad someone's taking us seriously," I say, thinking of the Officer Basilier and her dismissive tone.

We round the corner past the hedge maze, and the menagerie comes into view. Joe's pace quickens as he spots our destination, his massive 250-pound frame moving with surprising grace for such a giant dog.

Alfredo the giraffe spots us approaching and extends his elegant neck over the fence. His eyes, fringed with impossibly long lashes, fix on the basket in my hand.

We settle on a grassy knoll that gives us a perfect view of Alfredo's enclosure. Joe immediately plops down beside me, his eyes locked on the basket with laser focus. "Patience," I tell him, scratching behind his ears.

Maggie spreads out a checkered blanket and I set the basket in the center. Opening it reveals an array of delicacies: crusty baguettes, a selection of local cheeses, cold cuts arranged in a perfect spiral, a mason jar of velvety tomato soup, and small containers of what appears to be chocolate mousse.

I pull out three carrots that Chef Renauld included specifically for Alfredo. I told her I'm trying to get Alfredo on a healthier diet, and the first step is getting him used to vegetables. Rising to my feet, I approach his enclosure slowly, holding the carrots where he can see them.

"Hey, buddy," I say softly. Alfredo blinks those beautiful eyes and lowers his head toward me. I hold out the first carrot, and he turns his head away when he realizes it's not pasta.

"Alfredo," I say. "We're going to have to get over this. You can't *always* have carbs."

Begrudgingly, he takes the carrot with his prehensile tongue and gulps it down.

Joe whines from the blanket, clearly feeling that my attention is misplaced.

"Your dog is jealous of a giraffe!" Maggie calls out, laughing.

"Joe is jealous of anyone who gets food that isn't him," I reply, feeding Alfredo the last carrot before rejoining our picnic. I tear off a piece of baguette for Joe, who accepts it with exaggerated gratitude, as if he's been neglected for days instead of minutes.

I settle back onto the blanket and accept the plate Maggie has prepared for me. "So," I say between spoonfuls of the incredibly rich tomato soup, "we can check Lauda— the museum curator— and Pepper, the protestor— off our list of suspects to talk to. That leaves Lady Henrietta, Bitty, and Claude, who are all here at the castle."

Maggie nods, swallowing a bite of cheese. "You haven't met Lady Henrietta yet, have you?"

"Not officially," I say.

"You're in for a treat," Maggie says, rolling her eyes. "Lady Henrietta is what we politely call 'extremely passionate about her social media presence.' She's constantly having Bitty take photos of her for Instagram, trying to build her following."

Why does the Duke have such terrible family-members? I think to myself, remembering the visit from his cousins just a handful of weeks ago, one of whom turned out to be a killer.

"She wouldn't be the first member of the Royal family who's a murderer," I say. "Maybe she took the jewels to increase her coverage in the press."

"You're not wrong," Maggie agrees. "The Crown Jewels photoshoot was supposed to be Lady Henrietta's big viral moment. She's the Kim Kardashian of the Royal Family. And Bitty follows her lead in everything." Maggie takes a sip of sparkling water. "They're staying a suite on the top floor of the castle. And then there's Claude…"

"The Royal Jeweler," I nod, grabbing another olive from the charcuterie in front of me. "He seemed so nervous when he was being interviewed. I'm not sure the man has the courage to steal the Crown Jewels."

Maggie checks her watch. "All the same, I arranged for us to meet with Claude at two o'clock. I figured we'd talk to Lady Henrietta and Bitty first, then him."

"Good plan," I agree, leaning back on my elbows to enjoy the sunshine before it's time to return to sleuthing.

———

Lady Henrietta's suite is located in what Maggie calls "the plush wing" of Castle Atwood. As we approach the ornate double doors, I straighten my practical khaki shirt and suddenly feel very aware of the dog hair covering my pants. Joe, oblivious to any social anxiety, wags his tail enthusiastically beside me. Maggie, ever professional, smooths down her blazer and gives me a reassuring nod before knocking firmly on the door.

We wait. Muffled voices emerge from the room, followed by what sounds like an exasperated sigh. Finally, the door swings open to reveal a Bitty. Her blonde hair is back in a sleek bun, and she's wearing a pink velour tracksuit. She looks us up and down with an expression that suggests we're something unpleasant she's found on the bottom of her designer shoes.

"Bitty," I say, recognizing her at once.

"Yes?" she asks, one eyebrow arched so high it nearly disappears into her hairline. She looks at Maggie, the faintest bit of recognition crossing her face. "Margie, right?"

"Oh, um, it's *Maggie*," Maggie says pleasantly. "And this is Rebecca Orange, our animal expert. We'd like to speak with Lady Henrietta, please."

"She's busy with content creation. Come back later." Bitty begins to close the door.

I step forward quickly. "It's regarding the missing Crown Jewels. We won't take much of her time."

Bitty hesitates, then another voice calls from inside the suite. "Who is it, Bits?"

"The help," Bitty calls back, not taking her eyes off us. "They want to talk about the jewels."

There's a moment of silence, then: "Well, let them in, I suppose. But tell them to be quick. I have a live stream in twenty minutes."

Bitty rolls her eyes but steps back, opening the door wider. As I move to enter, Joe bounds forward excitedly, his massive form filling the doorway. Bitty lets out a shriek that could shatter crystal.

"What is THAT?" she demands, backing away from Joe as if he's a monster from a horror film.

"This is Joe," I say calmly. "My dog."

"That is *not* a dog," Bitty insists, clutching her tracksuit top. "That's a small horse with fur."

Joe, delighted by the attention, wags his tail harder and moves toward Bitty, his friendly eyes fixed on her face.

"He's very well-behaved," I assure her, though I make no move to hold him back. *It's good for Bitty to get a little dirty,* I think, smiling as she steps back to try and protect her pink track suit.

"Don't let it touch anything," Bitty hisses, side-stepping into the room. "These rugs are antiques."

We follow her into a suite that's straight out of a luxury magazine— if that magazine specialized in "royal quarters meets influencer paradise." The traditional furnishings are buried beneath ring lights, tripods, and what appears to be an entire professional-grade photography studio. Clothing racks line one wall, packed with outfits in every color imaginable. The other wall is dominated by a makeup station that would make a Hollywood star jealous.

In the center of this chaos, reclining on a chaise lounge, is

Lady Henrietta. She's scrolling through her phone, barely glancing up as we enter. Her hair extensions cascade over silk pillows, and her nails—at least two inches long and encrusted with tiny crystals—tap against her phone screen.

"Thank you for seeing us on such short notice," Maggie says, her tone perfectly professional.

Lady Henrietta finally looks up, her heavily made-up eyes sweeping over us with minimal interest. "You're here about the Crown Jewels, yes? Has there been a development?"

We both pull out our badges, and Maggie says smoothly, "We've been authorized to investigate on behalf of the Duke."

Lady Henrietta looks impressed despite herself. Bitty, meanwhile, has backed herself against the far wall, eyeing Joe with suspicion. Joe, sensing a challenge, ambles toward her with his most innocent expression.

"Your dog is *looking* at me," Bitty complains, pressing herself flatter against the wall.

"He's friendly," I say, hiding a smile as Joe sits directly in front of her, gazing up adoringly. A strand of drool drips from his mouth.

"If he drools on these shoes, I will sue," Bitty warns, lifting one foot to show off what I assume are extremely expensive pink heels.

I decide to redirect the conversation. "Lady Henrietta, could you walk us through the day the jewels disappeared? We understand you were planning a photoshoot with them."

Lady Henrietta sighs dramatically and sets down her phone. "It was meant to be show-stopping. The algorithm loves heritage content, and the Crown Jewels would have been my most-liked post ever." She gestures to Bitty. "Show them the concept board."

Bitty, still pressed against the wall with Joe watching her every move, points to a large mood board propped against a tripod. "I can't reach it with... *him* there."

"Joe, come," I command, and he reluctantly returns to my side, giving Bitty one last longing look filled with love.

Maggie examines the mood board, which is covered with images of jewels, crowns, and glamour shots of Lady Henrietta in various royal-inspired poses.

"We had it all planned," Lady Henrietta continues. "Claude was being an absolute pain about having to clean the jewels again that day, but I convinced him to let me wear the tiara for just a few photos. The rest would stay in their case. We were going to do a whole series—'Day in the Life of Royal Jewels' or something. Bitty had all the angles worked out. But Claude only gave us a few minutes with them. We took the photos and the jewels were still there when we left. I only realized they were missing out in the town square with everyone else."

"And where were you during this time, Bitty?" Maggie asks, turning to Lady Henrietta's lady-in-waiting.

"With Henrietta, obviously," Bitty replies, finally inching away from the wall now that Joe is occupied with sniffing a potted plant. "I was doing touch ups on her makeup. You can't rush perfection."

I nod toward a laptop open on a desk. "Do you mind if we see some of the photos you've posted recently? It might help us understand the timeline."

Lady Henrietta brightens at this request. "Bitty, show them my grid. The engagement has been insane lately."

Bitty moves to the laptop, giving Joe a wide berth, and pulls up an Instagram account with over five million followers. The page is filled with images of Lady Henrietta in various locations around Castle Atwood and beyond, each one more professionally staged than the last.

"I've been doing a castle series," Lady Henrietta explains, coming to stand beside us. Her perfume is overwhelming at this close range. Bitty clicks through pictures showing Lady Henrietta around the castle grounds— standing in the rose garden in a beautiful dress, lounging by the pool under an umbrella, even leaning next to Alfredo the giraffe at the menagerie.

A true friend to the animals, I think, noticing the way Alfredo seems to curl up his lip in the photo, as if he's repulsed by Lady Henrietta's presence.

"And what was Claude doing while you were taking pictures with the jewels?" I ask.

Lady Henrietta waves a dismissive hand. "Fussing with the display, I suppose. He's always fussing. The man needs a Xanax prescription."

"What about at your estate?" I ask, combing through my knowledge of the Crown Jewels. "How were the jewels maintained there, before you brought them to Atwood."

"Claude lived at the estate like the rest of my staff, and he kept them in the safe," Lady Henrietta waves a hand in the air as if the details are beneath her. "He made sure the jewels were cared for. They were in the dark all the time. We hardly ever saw them, and they weren't available to the public."

"And why did you decide to share them with Atwood?" Maggie asks, leaning in.

"Because the King and Queen ordered it," Lady Henrietta shrugs. "And they pointed out the jewels weren't helping my reputation by being locked in a safe all the time. They told me the Duke of Atwood thought it would bolster my image if I shared the jewels with the world. So I decided to grant them as a gift to the new museum."

"That was kind of you," I nod, considering what attention from the press means to a person like Lady Henrietta. "Although, one could argue that the disappearance of the jewels has gained even more attention than their presence. Wouldn't you agree?"

Bitty gasps, covering her mouth as if I've slapped her. Maggie's eyes widen and she shake her head at me as if to signal I should stop my line of questioning. Even Joe whimpers and lays down on the floor.

Lady Henrietta glares at me, and I immediately realize I've made a mistake.

You've really stepped in it now, Rebecca, I think to myself.

"Are you… accusing me of something?!" Lady Henrietta shrieks, her voice shrill.

"Not all, she was just—" Maggie tries to interject.

"Because, if you haven't noticed, I am of Royal blood, and do not deign to entertain conspiracy theories from commoners!"

"I was only—"

"You were only questioning my involvement in the disappearance of my own family's legacy?" Lady Henrietta says, her eyes narrowing as she shoves a finger in my direction. She shivers, seeming to shake away the implications of my questions. "You may go," she barks. "And what a pleasure this has been. You are so very welcome for the time! Bitty, show them out."

Bitty looks horrified at the prospect of having to approach Joe again, but dutifully moves toward the door, giving him a wide berth.

"Thank you," I say, realizing I've made a mess of things. "Joe, come."

My massive dog gets up and follows me, but not before giving Bitty one last soulful look that makes her press herself against the wall again.

As we exit the suite, I hear Lady Henrietta already on the phone. "You won't believe who just left. The Royal Investigators Jack hired. Yes, actual detectives! The impertinence. No, I didn't get footage, but I'm thinking we should do a follow-up vlog about the investigation… truly unconscionable how Royals are treated these days…"

The door closes behind us, cutting off her voice.

"Well, you really got to the bottom of that one," Maggie laughs as we head down the corridor.

"I'm so sorry!" I hiss, unable to believe my stupidity. "I was just—"

"Questioning her like everyone else," Maggie agrees. "It's alright, Rebecca. You're used to the Duke. Sadly, not all Royals are as open as Jack."

As we walk down the hallway to meet with Claude, I think about the jewels, and what it means to wear a crown on one's head. Maybe Henri was right, and commoners and Royals just don't mix.

And— if that's the case— Jack might as well be a fish to my bird.

CHAPTER
Nine

THIS SITTING room on the castle's bottom floor feels almost cozy despite the ornate ceiling and antique furniture. Claude perches on the edge of a velvet settee, repeatedly folding and unfolding a handkerchief between trembling fingers. His mustache twitches nervously as we enter. I recognize the anxious energy of someone in deep distress. Joe senses it too, his ears perking up with interest.

"Rebecca, I'd like you to meet Claude, the Royal Jeweler," Maggie says, her professional tone laced with genuine warmth. Maggie always roots for the underdogs of the world, and Claude certainly qualifies. "Claude, this is Rebecca Orange, the castle's animal expert."

Claude stands quickly, almost knocking over the small table in front of him. "P-p-pleased to meet you, M-Miss Orange," he stammers, extending a slightly damp hand that I shake firmly. "Though I w-wish it were under b-better circumstances."

His eyes dart to Joe, widening at the sight of my 250-pound companion. "And who is this magnificent animal?"

"This is Joe," I say, smiling as Claude takes a half-step

back. "Don't worry, he's the gentlest giant you'll ever meet. Joe, say hello nicely."

On cue, Joe sits, his enormous fluffy tail sweeping across the priceless rug. He tilts his head and offers a soft "woof" that sounds almost comically delicate coming from such a massive creature.

"He's v-very well trained," Claude observes, dabbing his forehead with his handkerchief.

"Please, let's all sit," Maggie suggests, gesturing to the arrangement of chairs and settees. "Tea should be arriving shortly."

I settle into a surprisingly comfortable armchair that probably costs more than my old apartment's yearly rent. Joe flops down at my feet, his huge form somehow managing to look elegant against the antique rug. Claude returns to perching on the edge of his seat, as if afraid to fully commit to the cushions.

"I understand you're here to ask me about the—" Claude says, his voice cracking slightly. "About the... the..."

"The theft of the Crown Jewels," Maggie supplies gently.

As if on cue, a castle attendant wheels in a tea cart laden with a silver service and what appears to be tiny sandwiches and cakes. I've never considered myself a "tea person," but castle life is quickly converting me. The attendant pours for each of us, then silently vanishes, closing the grand doors without a sound.

"The Duke has recently made Maggie and me Royal Investigators," I clarify, accepting my cup of tea with a nod of thanks to Maggie who hands it to me. "But we're just helping where we can. My expertise is animals, not jewels."

"Or thieves," Maggie adds with a small smile. "But Rebecca has a way of noticing things others might miss."

Claude's hands tremble as he attempts to lift his teacup. A small splash lands on his pristine trousers, and he hastily sets the cup down, reaching again for his handkerchief.

"I've f-failed," he blurts out suddenly, his voice tight with emotion. "Completely and utterly f-failed in my duty. Three generations of my family have served as Royal Jewelers, and I'm the one who l-lost the Crown Jewels."

I exchange a quick glance with Maggie. She gives me a subtle nod, encouraging me to take the lead in questioning him.

"How long have you been the Royal Jeweler, Claude?" I ask, keeping my tone conversational.

"T-twenty-three years," he answers, dabbing at his forehead again. "I apprenticed under my father from the age of f-fourteen, and took over when he retired twelve years ago."

"That's quite the dedication," I say, genuinely impressed. "Could you tell me a bit about what your job entails?"

Claude straightens slightly, professional pride momentarily overtaking his distress. "My primary duty is the preservation and maintenance of the royal collection. Each piece requires specific care. Temperature, humidity, cleaning methods... everything must be p-precise." His stutter lessens as he speaks about his work. "The diamond tiara, for instance, must be kept at exactly 68 degrees Fahrenheit with 40% humidity to prevent microscopic expansion and contraction of the metal settings."

Joe shifts at my feet, rolling slightly to expose his belly to the cool air. Claude's eyes flick to him nervously before continuing.

"The ruby necklace is particularly sensitive to oils from human skin, so I use specially treated cotton gloves when handling it, and clean it with a solution I m-mix myself from a family recipe." His voice gains confidence as he speaks about the technical aspects of his work. "And the ring— the diamond inside is flawless, but the setting is a soft gold that requires gentle handling. Even the small pearl bracelet requires regular cleaning to prevent the pearls from drying out."

"It sounds like incredibly meticulous work," I observe.

"It is my life's calling," Claude says simply, then his face crumples. "*Was* my life's calling."

His composure shatters, and he buries his face in his handkerchief. "I was so focused on keeping the jewels clean—on maintaining the perfect environment. I never... I never thought..." He takes a shaky breath. "I was so concerned with preservation that I didn't properly consider security. I trusted that Anthony had that aspect handled."

At the mention of Anthony, Joe's ears prick up. He's only met the guard briefly, but my dog never forgets a person.

"How is Anthony?" Claude asks suddenly, looking up with red-rimmed eyes. "I've been so overcome with worry about him. Is there any news?"

Maggie shakes her head gently. "He still hasn't regained consciousness. The doctors say the blow to his head was severe, but they're hopeful he might wake up."

"It's all my fault," Claude moans. "If I had been more vigilant..."

"Anthony is a trained security professional," Maggie reassures him. "No one blames you for focusing on your area of expertise."

I watch Claude carefully as he twists his handkerchief into a tight knot. There's genuine distress in his eyes, but I can't help wondering if it's primarily for the jewels, for Anthony, or for himself.

"Can you tell us about the day the jewels were taken?" I ask, setting down my teacup.

Claude nods miserably. "Lady Henrietta had requested access to them for a special photoshoot. Something about 'royal heritage content' for her social media. Her grandmother—the Queen—approved it, so I allowed her to see them. She'd been around them for years, after all, considering they were kept safely at her estate. She never showed the slightest interest in them until now—"

"That must have been stressful," I prompt, hoping to get him talking more.

"Lady Henrietta is..." Claude pauses, clearly searching for diplomatic wording. "She is very enthusiastic and perhaps not as... careful as I would prefer. I didn't let the jewels out of my sight the entire time. Not for a m-moment."

Joe stretches and shifts positions, laying his massive head on my foot. The weight is comforting, grounding.

"I insisted on proper lighting to prevent heat damage, supervised the handling of each piece, and personally secured them in their velvet cushions afterward." Claude's mustache quivers with indignation. "When she was finished with her pictures, I locked them right back into the case."

"Claude, this is very important," I say, leaning forward. "Are you *sure* you locked the case?"

"I'm sure," he nods. Then, he hesitates. "But… what if I didn't? Perhaps I'm wrong. Maybe it's my fault."

"Did you see Anthony at all that morning?"

"Anthony was there when I left to get my coffee." Claude pulls out a fresh handkerchief from his pocket.

"And when did you discover the jewels were missing?" Maggie asks gently.

"In the town square, with everyone else. I didn't think to check beneath the cloth before we wheeled them outside because it was simply inconceivable that they'd be missing!" He looks up at us, eyes wide with despair. "I expect I'll be fired. The Royal Jeweler who lost the Crown Jewels can hardly remain employed. But I d-don't know what I'll do. Where I'll go. These jewels have been my entire life." His voice drops to a whisper. "I have failed at the one thing I was born to do."

And I thought I felt bad when I got fired from the San Diego Safari Park, I think to myself. Claude's loss seems much bigger, given his family legacy.

Joe whines softly, sensing the man's distress. He lifts his

head and looks at Claude with those soulful eyes that have always been able to read emotions better than most humans.

"Do you— k-k-know about the history of the Crown Jewels, Miss Orange?" Claude says, looking so deep into my eyes I'm afraid he might learn my every secret.

"I know the Queen loved the man who gave them to her, but couldn't marry him because he wasn't Royal," I say, unable to keep the trace of sadness from my voice.

Claude clucks his tongue at me, forgetting his own pain when he sees my own. "You've misunderstood the story, then."

"I have?"

"The Crown Jewels don't represent the distance between Royals and commoners," Claude answers. "Th-they represent the best of us. When her love died at sea, the Queen made the jewels the official symbol of the monarchy. Because the man who gave them to her had the heart of a true Monrovian. The jewels are about how we are *alike*— not the ways in which we are *different*. They represent a love that transcends station. They symbolize the lengths Monrovians are willing to go to do what is best for their country." He sniffles again, his face suddenly flushing. "And I— I've lost them!" He blows his nose into his handkerchief.

"This wasn't your fault, Claude," I say, standing up. Joe rises beside me, his massive form unfolding like an origami sculpture. "We *will* get to the bottom of this. And I'm sorry about what you're going through."

I mean it sincerely. Whatever happened with the jewels, this man is clearly suffering.

Claude nods numbly, not looking up. "If there's anything else I can help…"

Maggie places a gentle hand on his shoulder. "We'll be in touch, Claude. Try to rest if you can."

We leave him sitting there, a small, broken figure in an

enormous room full of priceless antiques. As the doors close behind us, I glance at Maggie.

"Well?" she asks quietly as we walk down the hallway, Joe trotting between us.

"He's genuinely devastated," I say. "That much is obvious."

"But?"

"But devastation doesn't equal innocence." I run my hand through Joe's thick fur as we walk. "People can feel guilty for all sorts of reasons. Maybe he feels responsible because he failed to prevent the theft. Or *maybe* he feels guilty because he was involved. The thing about guilt," I say, "is that it often looks the same whether you're blaming yourself for something you didn't do or something you did. We can feel bad for him, but we can't rule him out yet."

Joe woofs softly in agreement, or perhaps he's just ready for his afternoon walk.

"Did it bother you?" Maggie asks. "Hearing the story about the jewels again?"

"A little," I admit, although I don't want to say why.

"Well, maybe this will cheer you up," Maggie pulls out her tablet, opening up an email with a calendar invitation before passing it to me. "I've been asked to set up a dinner tomorrow night with you and the Duke at *Le Petit Scone*."

My breath catches in my throat at the thought of a dinner with Jack.

"That is, if your schedule is clear?" Maggie winks at me, a teasing edge to her voice.

"It is now!" I laugh, still thinking about what Claude said about the Crown Jewels representing the best of us.

CHAPTER
Ten

TALK ABOUT FEELING LIKE ROYALTY, I think. The Duke of Atwood has cleared out an entire bakery for our dinner. *Le Petit Scone* glows with candlelight, the smell of fresh bread and pastries hanging in the air like the world's most delicious perfume. Joe sits at my feet, eyeing a display case of croissants with the intense focus of a bomb squad technician. Outside, the cobblestone streets of the village are quiet, save for the occasional click of what I'm pretty sure are paparazzi cameras. The windows have been blocked so that the reporters can't see us, but they're still determined to try to get a scoop.

This is definitely a date, isn't it? My stomach flips as the Duke pulls out my chair.

"Thank you for joining me tonight, Rebecca," he says, his voice warm. "I thought you might enjoy seeing Henri's place without the usual crowd."

"It's beautiful," I say, taking in the quaint charm of the bakery. Heavy velvet curtains have been drawn across the windows, creating a cocoon of privacy and blocking out the reporters outside. The tables—normally packed with morning customers—have been cleared away except for ours. It's covered by a white tablecloth and flickering candles.

"Henri wasn't thrilled about the dog," the Duke whispers, leaning in conspiratorially. "But I told him Joe is practically royalty in his own right."

On cue, Joe lets out a massive sigh and flops onto the hardwood floor, taking up about as much space as a small pony.

"He promises to be on his best behavior," I say, though Joe's eyes haven't left the pastry case. "Don't you, buddy?"

Joe's tail thumps once against the floor, which I choose to interpret as a solemn oath. A waiter— thankfully not Henri— emerges from the kitchen, carrying two glasses of deep red wine. He places them before us with a bow so deep I worry he might topple over.

"Your Grace," he murmurs to the Duke, then nods at me with a cautious, "Madame."

I can feel him taking in my simple black dress and minimal jewelry—probably wondering what on earth I'm doing here with the Duke of Atwood. *Don't worry,* I think, *I'm wondering the same thing.*

"Henri has prepared a special menu tonight," the Duke explains as the waiter retreats. "His famous twisted braid cake for dessert, of course, but he's also making his grandmother's cassoulet."

"I'm honored," I say, though based on my limited interactions with Henri, I suspect the honor is grudgingly given. The few times I've stopped in for coffee, he's watched me like I might pocket the silverware.

Jack takes a sip of his wine. "Henri's family has been baking in this spot for over three hundred years. The recipe for that twisted braid cake is older than the United States."

"He mentioned that," I say. "Several times."

Jack laughs. "He doesn't fully trust Americans. Or change. Or anything that happened after 1850."

There's another click from outside, followed by a muffled thump against the curtains. Jack's smile falters.

"I'm sorry about that," he says, nodding toward the window. "The press has been particularly persistent lately."

"Because of me?" I ask, suddenly self-conscious.

He shakes his head. "Because of the jewels. Their disappearance has everyone in a frenzy. The public is fascinated because jewels have a romantic history that makes them especially beloved."

A romantic history that makes this date pointless, I think to myself before shrugging off the feeling. *Stay in the moment, Rebecca.*

The waiter returns with our first course: delicate mushroom tartlets with fresh herbs. The scent makes my mouth water immediately.

"This looks amazing," I say.

Jack smiles and raises his glass. "To new experiences."

I clink my glass against his. "To new experiences."

We eat in comfortable silence for a moment, the tartlets melting on my tongue. Joe shifts at my feet, resting his huge head on my foot as if to say, "Don't forget I'm here."

"I'd slip you a piece if it wouldn't get us both banished from Monrovia," I whisper to Joe.

"How is he adjusting to castle life?" Jack asks.

"He loves the grounds. Not so fond of the suits of armor—they make him nervous."

"I understand completely," Jack says with a laugh. "They terrified me as a child. I used to think they'd come alive at night and roam the halls."

There's another flash outside, and Jack's smile fades. He sets down his fork with a sigh.

"I was so— disappointed— that our last dinner at the castle felt overly formal. And I was so hoping to get some privacy tonight. Sometimes I think my perfect life would be one completely away from the public eye."

"What would that look like?" I ask, genuinely curious about this man who seems both comfortable with and constrained by his position.

He considers this, tilting his head. "A small stone house somewhere remote. Books lining every wall. A garden I tend myself. No photographers, no formal dinners, no constant scrutiny." His eyes soften. "Just peace and the freedom to be myself rather than what everyone expects the Duke to be."

The waiter appears again, removing our plates and replacing them with bowls of fragrant cassoulet. The rich aroma of beans, duck, and sausage fills the air. Joe's nose twitches appreciatively.

"And what about you, Rebecca?" Jack asks as we begin our main course. "What would your perfect life be?"

I take a bite of the cassoulet to buy myself time. It's heavenly—rich and savory with herbs that remind me of the Monrovian hillsides I've grown to love on my morning walks with Joe.

"I've never really thought about it," I lie, then catch myself. "No, that's not true. I have thought about it. I just never thought it was possible."

Jack leans forward, his eyes intent on mine. "Tell me."

"A small cottage," I begin, suddenly feeling vulnerable. "Nothing fancy, but with huge grounds. Enough space for all kinds of animals—rescues, mostly, that I work to rehabilitate. Somewhere quiet, much like you— I like to be away from crowds."I take another sip of wine, fortifying myself. "I'd have my morning coffee on a porch watching the sunrise, with Joe and whatever other creatures have found their way to me. I'd work with animals who need rehabilitation, and in the evenings, I'd sit by a fire." I pause, then add without thinking, "I'd want very few humans around— maybe just one man I can tolerate would be enough."

The words hang in the air between us. Jack's eyes haven't left mine, and there's something in them I can't quite read.

"I would be honored to be considered for that position," he says quietly.

My heart does a little flip in my chest. Okay, now I'm absolutely certain this is a date. The Duke of Atwood—Jack—just essentially said he could see himself in my imaginary future. With me. In a cottage. The thought makes me dizzy.

"If the bar is tolerating the bloke, I should think I can pass the test," Jack smiles.

"I know Joe would approve," I manage to say, glancing down at my dog, who has rolled onto his back, enormous paws in the air, completely unconcerned with our romantic tension.

Jack laughs, breaking the intensity of the moment. "High praise indeed. His approval is not easily earned"

"It's a huge compliment that he likes you so much. He's an excellent judge of character. Better than me, sometimes."

The waiter appears again, clearing our dishes with silent efficiency. In the kitchen, I catch a glimpse of Henri watching us through the pass-through window, his mustache twitching with what might be disapproval.

"Can I ask you something?" I say as we wait for dessert.

"Of course." Jack's attention is fully on me, making me feel both important and slightly nervous.

"I've fallen in love with Monrovia," I start. "The land-scapes, the food, the history—it's all so beautiful. But there's something I've been curious about since I heard the story of the Crown Jewels."

Jack's expression shifts subtly. "Oh?"

"The jewels were given to a Queen by a man who loved her, but they couldn't be together because he wasn't royal," I say. "Is that still the law here? Can a Royal ever be with a commoner?"

Jack blinks, and I can see a flush creeping up his neck. For the first time tonight, he seems flustered.

"That's—well, it's complicated," he begins. "Historically,

yes, there were strict laws preventing such unions. But modern Monrovia has evolved. The legal prohibitions have been removed, though tradition still holds considerable sway in certain circles."

"Certain circles like … ?" I press gently.

Jack runs a finger around the rim of his water glass. "My aunt and uncle—the King and Queen—are progressive in many ways, but they're also deeply committed to tradition. They've given me considerable freedom with Castle Atwood, allowing me to open it to the public and modernize its role in the community. But when it comes to personal matters..." He trails off.

"They have expectations," I finish for him.

He nods, looking relieved that I understand. "Yes. But I've never been particularly good at meeting expectations simply because they exist. I'm not sure if you've noticed, but I'm most committed to disappointing them at every possible turn."

There's something in his tone that gives me a flutter of hope. Before I can respond, the waiter returns with two slices of the famous twisted braid cake, studded with golden raisins and olives—an odd combination that somehow works beautifully.

"This is—" I begin, but I'm interrupted by a soft fluttering sound from above.

Jack looks up first. A piece of paper drifts down from one of the ceiling vents, floating like a feather until it lands directly on our table between the cake slices.

Jack picks it up, his brow furrowing as he reads. His face drains of color.

"What is it?" I ask, setting down my fork.

Without a word, he hands me the paper. In block letters, it reads: "STOP LOOKING FOR THE JEWELS: OR ELSE."

"What?" I whisper, glancing around the empty bakery. "Who would—"

My words are cut off by a soft hissing sound. Suddenly, white smoke begins pouring from the same ceiling vent where the note appeared. It billows down in thick clouds, quickly filling the small bakery.

"Jack!" I call out, but the smoke is already so dense I can barely see him across the table. Joe leaps to his feet beside me, his bark deep and alarmed.

I reach out, trying to find Jack's hand, but the smoke is disorienting. There's a clanging sound as a candlestick topples over, and suddenly the table goes up in flames. Joe barks at my feet, his raspy voice an alarm bell. My eyes sting, and my throat tightens. Through the thickening haze, I hear chairs scraping against the floor and confused shouts from the kitchen.

"Rebecca!" Jack's voice sounds distant, though he must be only feet away. "Rebecca, stay where you are!"

But the smoke keeps coming, and panic rises in my chest like a tide. Joe presses against my legs, his body tense and protective. Through watering eyes, I strain to see the Duke's silhouette, but he's impossible to find in the cloud of smoke and haze. The air burns my lungs, and I put my sleeve over my mouth, trying to catch my breath.

My heart pounds as I realize I can't tell which way leads to the door. The smoke has transformed the charming bakery into a disorienting void, and all I can feel is Joe's warm body against mine and the cold grip of fear closing around my throat.

I'm going to die on my date, I think, bewildered at the idea. *And I didn't even get to have dessert!*

CHAPTER
Eleven

SMOKE CLAWS at my throat as I stumble forward, arms outstretched in the murky darkness of *Le Petit Scone*. My eyes sting, tears streaming down my face as I try to blink away the blur. Somewhere ahead, I know the Duke is there— I heard his voice calling out seconds ago—but the thick, rolling clouds of smoke have swallowed everything.

Then, a hand closes around my arm.

"Jack?" I choke out, the smoke making my voice raspy and thin.

Jack moves his hand down my arm, interlacing my fingers in his firm, warm, grip. Even in this chaos, I can feel the distinct shape of his signet ring pressing against my skin.

"Rebecca! Stay close!" His voice sounds strained but steady, anchoring me in the disorienting haze.

"Joe?!" I shout, suddenly afraid that I've lost him. But then, a bark emerges from the a few feet up a head.

"He's here, Rebecca!" Jack shouts. "He's in front of me! He's leading us to the door. Don't let go of my hand!"

I tighten my grip, relief washing over me. The bakery that just minutes ago smelled of warm bread and sweet pastries now reeks of acrid smoke that burns my nostrils with each desperate breath. Around us, the display cases and counters have transformed into shadowy obstacles in a maze that was once familiar.

Joe's frantic barking cuts through the roar of the fire. His deep, resonant alert bark— the one he uses only in emergencies— guides us like a sonic beacon through the smoke towards the entrance.

"Almost there!" the Duke shouts. "He's a genius."

"Joe?!" I shout.

Another series of barks answers me, closer to the front of the bakery now. Two hundred and fifty pounds of dog intuition might just save our lives today.

"Your dog," Jack says between coughs, "is smarter than some of my advisors."

Even in this moment of danger, I feel a small bubble of laughter rise in my chest, though it quickly turns into another coughing fit. The smoke is getting thicker, swirling around us in angry gray tendrils. Each breath feels like inhaling tiny needles.

Jack pulls me forward, his hand steady in mine. "Keep your head low," he instructs, and I comply, hunching down as we move through the thickening smoke. I can barely see my own feet now, and the only thing keeping panic at bay is the reassuring pressure of the Duke's hand around mine.

The temperature rises as we move toward Joe's barking. Sweat trickles down my back, my clothes sticking uncomfortably to my skin. My lungs burn with each shallow breath, and my eyes water so badly I might as well be walking blind.

"Almost there," Jack encourages, though I'm not sure how he can tell. The smoke has turned the world into a uniform gray void.

Something crashes behind us—a shelf collapsing, maybe, or part of the ceiling giving way. I flinch at the sound, and Jack's hand tightens around mine.

"Don't look back," he says firmly. "Just forward."

Joe's barking has taken on a frantic quality now. He's scared, but he's staying put, guiding us to safety like a furry lighthouse in a storm.

We shuffle forward a few more steps until Jack suddenly stops. "We've reached the door," he says, relief evident in his voice despite the strain.

"Joe!" I shout, bending down to grab Joe's collar. He pushes his body close to mine, whining in fear as he practically tries to leap into my arms.

I reach out with my free hand and feel the outline of the front door. The glass is hot to the touch, but not scorching. The fire hasn't reached this far yet, but the smoke has made it impossible to see the exit mechanisms. The Duke tries the metal handle, but the door doesn't move. He presses against it with his body, but it stays shut.

"The heat's melted the door frame!" Jack says. "Rebecca. I need you to get down and cover your head. Close your eyes tightly. Cover Joe's face."

"What are you—"

"Trust me," he interrupts. "Please."

There's something in his voice—a mixture of earnestness and genuine concern—that makes me trust him. I drop to a crouch, covering my head with my arms, eyes squeezed shut. Joe tucks his face beneath my arms, and we huddle together — waiting.

For a moment, there's only the sound of our labored breathing and Joe's continued barking. Then comes a new sound—fabric wrapping around something, followed by Jack grunting with effort.

The smashing of glass explodes through the smoky air, shards tinkling down like deadly rain. The sound is so sudden and violent that I gasp, inadvertently sucking in a lungful of smoke that sends me into another coughing fit.

"You broke the glass," I realize aloud, understanding dawning through my smoke-addled brain.

"Stay down," Jack warns, and I feel glass fragments patter against my back and arms. Most are small, but as we step through the threshold, I feel a sharp sting on my forearm that I ignore for now. I turn around and whistle at Joe, who leaps through the glass and onto the cobblestone street.

A rush of fresh air suddenly cuts through the smoke, sweet and clean. I gulp it greedily, still hunched over.

"Clear a path," Jack calls out to someone outside. Then his hands are on my shoulders. "Can you stand? We need to move quickly."

I nod, though I'm not sure Jack can see me through the haze. His hands slip beneath my arms, helping me to my feet. Together, we stumble toward the newly created exit.

"Watch the glass," Jack warns, guiding me carefully. I feel the crunch of fragments beneath my shoes as we move.

Then we're through, emerging from the smoke-filled bakery into the cool evening. The sudden transition is jarring, the fresh air almost painful as it fills my deprived lungs. I double over in a coughing fit, my eyes still streaming tears.

When I finally straighten up, wiping my face with my hands, I'm struck by the scene around us. What seems like half the village has gathered in the square. Ambulances with flashing lights have pulled up, their sirens cutting through the morning air. Paramedics rush forward with oxygen masks and blankets.

And cameras. So many cameras.

"Your Highness! Miss Orange!" voices call out from all directions, flashes popping like lightning strikes. The local press has materialized as if by magic, capturing every moment of our disheveled escape.

It's then that I realize Jack and I are still holding hands, our fingers intertwined like lovers caught in a secret rendezvous rather than two people who just escaped a burning building.

I spot Zacharia among the photographers, his camera

aimed directly at us, a satisfied smile playing at the corners of his mouth as he captures frame after frame. Of course he'd be here—probably arrived before the fire department.

"Your highness! Is this confirmation of your relationship with Miss Orange?" someone shouts.

"Rebecca! How long have you been secretly dating the Duke?" calls another.

Beside me, Jack straightens to his full height, his royal bearing asserting itself even with soot smudged across his face and his usually impeccable clothes in disarray. He doesn't let go of my hand.

"This is hardly the time," he says with remarkable composure. "The fire—"

"Under control, Your Highness," a firefighter reports, approaching us with respectful efficiency. "We've got the kitchen staff out through the back."

Joe pushes through the crowd, making his way to my side, his golden coat now streaked with gray from the smoke. He nudges my free hand with his nose, and I stroke his head reassuringly.

"You're a hero, buddy," I tell him, my voice raw and scratchy.

A paramedic approaches with oxygen masks. "You both need to be checked," she says firmly, apparently unintimidated by royal presence.

As she hands me a mask, her eyes widen. "Miss, your arm!"

I look down to see a dark stain spreading across my sleeve. A piece of glass must have cut deeper than I realized during our escape. As I stare at the blood soaking through the fabric, a strange lightheadedness washes over me.

Oh no. Not now, I think, trying to steady myself. I've never been good with blood—especially my own. The sight of the red stain expanding across my arm sends the world tilting sideways. The sounds around me—the cameras clicking, Joe barking, the paramedic's concerned voice—all begin to fade into a distant buzz.

I'm struck by the mental image of a ship sinking, except the ship is me. *Brace yourselves everyone! She's going down.*

"Rebecca?" I hear Jack's voice, suddenly anxious. His hand tightens around mine.

The last thing I'm aware of is the Duke's strong arms catching me as my knees buckle. Camera flashes explode like stars behind my eyelids. Something soft and warm—Joe, probably—presses against my side.

What an embarrassing way to die, I think. Then everything goes black.

CHAPTER

Twelve

FOR A SECOND, the smell of alcohol makes me think I've been taken to a bar. But then I realize it's not alcohol at all—just the antiseptic sheen of a hospital. My eyes blink open to fluorescent lights that seem impossibly bright, making me wince. My brain has been replaced by cotton. *Where am I?* The beeping of a monitor somewhere to my left answers the question before I can fully form it.

Hospital. I'm in a hospital. But why?

A heavy warmth presses against my side, familiar and comforting. I tilt my head to find Joe's massive form somehow wedged onto the narrow hospital bed beside me, his golden coat spilling over the white sheets like honey. His eyes open as soon as I move, as if he's been waiting for me to wake up. His tail thumps against the mattress in a gentle rhythm.

"Hey, buddy," I whisper, my voice rough. I try to lift my hand to pet him, but a sharp twinge of pain stops me. Looking down, I see my right hand is wrapped in white gauze. The sight triggers a flash of memory—smoke filling *Le Petit Scone*, the crash of something falling, sharp pain as

I...what? The memory slips away like water through cupped hands.

"She's awake," a voice says—warm, cultured, with just a hint of relief that makes something flutter in my chest.

I turn my head to see the Duke of Atwood rising from a chair by the window. His salt-and-pepper hair is slightly mussed, as if he's been running his hands through it with worry. Behind him stands Maggie, her usually immaculate braids looking a bit frayed at the edges, dark circles under her eyes.

"Welcome back to the land of the living," Maggie says with a smile that doesn't quite hide her concern. "You gave us quite a scare."

"What happened?" I ask, trying to push myself up to sitting. Joe shifts to accommodate me, pressing his warm bulk against my side in silent support.

The Duke steps closer to the bed, his hands in his pockets. "You fainted at *Le Petit Scone*. Do you remember?"

I close my eyes, trying to piece together the fragmented memories. "There was smoke... and a loud noise. You broke the glass..." I shake my head. "It was the blood on my arm. I've never been good with blood."

"Not entirely" the Duke says, his voice gentle. "You cut your arm from the glass and lost some blood, but they were able to give you a transfusion. So I'm afraid it wasn't just anxiety that made you faint."

"That's helpful to know," I nod. "Much less embarrassing to have an actual medical reason for collapsing."

"The Duke insisted on bringing you here rather than just the local clinic," Maggie says, giving him a meaningful look that makes him shift his weight from one foot to the other. "He practically carried you to the ambulance himself."

I glance at the Duke, who suddenly seems very interested in the pattern of the hospital blanket. "Thank you," I tell him, meaning it.

"I shouldn't have broken the glass in the door—" he says, shaking his head. "You were hurt because I was so reckless."

"You're right. Next time definitely let us die in the fire," I agree.

The Duke laughs. "You give me too much grave."

"Rebecca," Maggie says, concerned. "Someone set off some kind of smoke device in the bakery. You were targeted."

The word "targeted" sends a chill through me. "Henri? Is he okay?"

"He's fine," Maggie assures me quickly. "Shaken up, but not hurt. He's already back at the bakery, cleaning up and planning the restoration. Says it'll take more than a little smoke to keep him from his ovens."

I smile at that, picturing the determined old baker kneading his dough with the same ferocity he brings to everything. "I'm starting to think my castle animal expert job is more dangerous than advertised," I say, attempting a joke to lighten the mood.

"It must be whoever took the jewels, don't you think?" the Duke says, running a hand through his hair in a gesture I'm beginning to recognize as a sign of stress.

"That's an investigation in progress, Your Highness," I feign an official tone. "I'm afraid we can't share information on the case until we've made a determination."

"That's what I get for empowering the two of you," the Duke winks at Maggie, a smile tugging at the edge of his mouth.

Maggie checks her watch. "The doctor should be back soon with your discharge papers. They want to keep you for a few more hours of observation, but you should be able to go home tonight."

Home. The castle. It's strange how quickly that massive stone building has begun to feel like a place I belong.

"Rebecca, I'm so sorry our evening was interrupted once again," the Duke says, sitting closer on the edge of the bed.

Maggie takes the hint and pretends to examine a poster on the wall. "It seems every time I try to see you we're interrupted, and I'd so love to—"

Just then, the door to my room swings open, and I expect to see a doctor in a white coat. Instead, Officer Basilier strides in, her petite form somehow filling the space with authority. Her uniform is crisp and unwrinkled despite the late hour, her expression stern as she surveys the room.

"Maggie. Miss Orange," she says with a curt nod. "Good to see you conscious." She scans Jack. "Your Highness."

"Officer Basilier," the Duke acknowledges, his tone cooling several degrees. "I didn't realize the local police had jurisdiction in hospital rooms."

"We have jurisdiction anywhere a crime has been committed against a civilian," she replies without looking at him. Her focus is entirely on me. "How much do you remember about the incident at *Le Petit Scone*?"

"She's hardly ready to be interviewed now!" The Duke objects, but I wave his concern away.

Joe grumbles low in his throat, sensing the tension in the room. I place my uninjured hand on his massive head to quiet him.

"It's fine. Not much," I admit. "Smoke, a loud noise, then nothing until I woke up here."

Officer Basilier pulls out a small notebook and flips it open. "We've completed our preliminary investigation of the scene. The smoke came from a smoke bomb, the kind used in theatrical productions or paintball games. Harmless, but effective at causing confusion. It was knocking over the candlesticks that created the actual fire."

"So whoever did this wasn't trying to hurt anyone," Maggie concludes.

"It appears that way," Officer Basilier agrees reluctantly. "The device was placed near the back of the shop, away from customers. The note you found was dropped through the vents. The timing—in the evening, when the two of *you* were the only guests—also suggests the perpetrator wanted to minimize harm."

"They just wanted to scare us," I say slowly.

"To scare *you*, specifically," Officer Basilier corrects, her sharp eyes meeting mine. "I thought I asked you to stop investigating the disappearance of the crown jewels. Perhaps now you can see why."

"She's acting on my authority—" Jack offers, but Officer Basilier cuts him off.

"Your authority means nothing here—"

"I'm only asking questions," I say, keeping my voice even. "Is that a crime in Monrovia?"

"No, but obstruction of justice is." She snaps her notebook closed. "This is precisely why I warned you against playing detective, Miss Orange. You're not trained for this work. You've put yourself in danger and complicated an official investigation."

"That's enough, Officer," the Duke says quietly, but with the kind of authority that makes everyone in the room straighten up slightly. "Miss Orange is recovering from an injury. I stand by my initial assertion— this can wait."

Officer Basilier's jaw tightens, but she nods stiffly. "Of course, Your Grace." The formality sounds almost like an insult in her mouth. "I'll need a full statement from Miss Orange once she's discharged. And I strongly recommend that castle staff leave the investigation to those qualified to conduct it."

"Duly noted," the Duke says, holding the door open pointedly.

Officer Basilier gives me one last measuring look before she leaves, her boots clicking sharply against the hospital floor. The tension in the room eases like air from a punctured balloon once she's gone. Joe huffs his disapproval at the offi-cer's departure, and I can't help but agree with the sentiment.

"Whoever did this is getting nervous," I say to Maggie, unable to contain my excitement. "We're close to finding the jewels,"

"And look where it's gotten you," Jack says, gesturing at the hospital bed.

"A nice nap and some quality time with my dog?" I smile up at him. "I've had worse days. I spent fifteen years working with predators that could kill me with one swipe," I remind him. "I know how to handle risk. Maggie and I are cracking this case wide open. Don't let Officer Basilier scare you off."

He laughs, a warm sound that fills the sterile hospital room with life. "If there's one thing the Royal Family of Monrovia doesn't do, it's scare easily. If you're determined to continue, then you have my full support."

I nod. "Maggie, you're still in?"

"Am I still in?" Maggie gasps, sitting on the edge of the bed. "This is more exciting than *ever*. This might be our best case yet."

The Duke reaches out and gives my unbandaged hand a gentle squeeze. "Well then, Miss Orange—or should I say, *Detective* Orange— I'll go let the front desk know you're alert and ready to go home. Let's get you out of here. It seems you have a mystery to solve." He adds softly, "Although, I am quite sad our dinner was interrupted."

"We'll have to make it up again," I tell him. "It's kind of our thing now, isn't it? We just always owe each other one more."

"To one more," Jack smiles before exiting.

Joe barks once, as if in agreement. Despite the throbbing in my hand and the lingering headache from my concussion, I feel a surge of excitement. Someone tried to frighten me off, but they don't know who they're dealing with. Rebecca

Orange doesn't scare easily either. And with the Duke's support, Joe's loyalty, and my own stubborn determination, I'm going to find out exactly who's behind all this—smoke bombs be damned.

CHAPTER
Thirteen

SUNLIGHT STREAMS through the windows of *Cafe de Flore*, catching on the delicate flower arrangements that decorate each table. My bandaged hand throbs slightly as I reach for my coffee cup, but the pain is worth it for the lavender latte that's become my morning addiction. Across from me, Maggie leans forward, her blonde braids swinging as she eyes my injury with concern, while Joe lounges contentedly at my feet, occasionally lifting his massive head to accept a scratch from passing waitstaff who've already fallen in love with him.

"That's not getting infected, is it?" Maggie says, stirring her rosehip tea. "Are you sure you don't need to see a doctor again? The castle physician could—"

"It's fine," I interrupt, flexing my fingers carefully beneath the bandage. "Just a few cuts from the broken glass. It's healing perfectly. I barely remember the night." *Except for how handsome the Duke looked.*

Joe shifts at my feet, his warm bulk pressing against my ankles as if to remind me he's there, ready to protect me from any further threats. I reach down to scratch behind his ears, grateful for his steady presence.

"Well, thank goodness you're both okay!" Maggie says, setting down her spoon with a decisive clink. "When I heard someone attacked you two at *Le Petite Scone*, I nearly had a heart attack." She puts her hand on mine, her eyes wide with feeling. "You've become one of my best friends, Rebecca. I couldn't imagine—"

"I feel the same," I tell her, grateful to have a friend who cares about me. I clear my throat, trying to push away the tenderness. "Besides," I add sternly. "Who would I investigate with? I need the Watson to my Sherlock."

Maggie smiles at me, the leans in, whispering. "Okay, so now that you feel well enough, I have to know… what do you think this means? I mean, the note you got telling you to stop investigating? The smoke bomb?" Maggie sits back in her chair, pretending to pout. "I'm actually a little offended the attacker didn't come after me too! I'm part of this investigation as well, if they hadn't noticed."

"Don't worry," I sigh. "You may be next." I take another sip of my tea, thinking about our next move. "Should we go through our suspects again?"

"Yes," Maggie agrees. "I've been working with Lauda to get the museum ready for the ground opening and I've used the time to observe her, so I have more to report. She's brilliant but intense. She told me her biggest dream is to be one of these world-famous scholars who gets book deals and goes on talk shows. This is a woman aiming for the stars."

"That's— great, but also a little much, isn't it?"

Maggie shrugs. "It's good for me because she's always on top of things. It's made planning the grand opening a breeze. She's been working around the clock to make sure everything's perfect."

"That doesn't sound like someone who would ruin her own event. Unless… maybe she's in debt from student loans?"

Maggie considers this. "I suppose it's possible."

"And what about Claude? Any updates from him while I was out last night?"

"He's just been moping around," Maggie answers. Then, she gasps. "But Lady Henrietta posted on social media last night!" She takes out her phone and opens an app, showing me a picture of Lady Henrietta and Bitty, standing in front of the empty case where the jewels used to sit. "She has no shame. She's been milking the disappearance of the Crown Jewels for all she can."

"Hardly sympathetic," I say. "But also… it doesn't make her a murderer." My brain scans all options, trying to determine if there's any rock I've left unturned. But Maggie beats me to the punch.

"Oh my goodness," she says, slapping her forehead. "Rebecca, I've just realize— I forgot to tell you the most important thing."

"What?"

"You were so tired last night and I completely forgot in all the chaos."

My heart races. From Maggie's tone, I can tell this is big. "Watson, you better tell me now before—"

"Anthony, the guard, is awake!" She says. Then, her face falls. "But— there's a bad part—"

"What's the bad part?"

There's a long pause. Then, Maggie adds: "The bad part is, he doesn't remember anything. The police already interviewed him and he told them he was using the bathroom when he was hit over the head with something. He didn't even know it was a statue. He just remembers falling and then it was lights out."

"I can relate to that," I say, thinking about my fainting spell last night.

"So it seems Anthony won't be any help," Maggie shrugs. "But…" She leans in, eyes sparkling with excitement. "Today I have to get the museum ready for the grand opening. And I could use a couple of assistants. Hopefully assistants that break off and use the time for sleuthing. Today we'll set you loose and who knows— maybe you'll find something we missed last time."

I smile down at Joe.

"Get your nose, ready, buddy."

———

Moments later, we exit Cafe de Flore and stroll down the cobblestone streets, Joe padding contentedly beside me. Maggie chatters about the museum as we walk, but I'm distracted by the charm of Atwood village. Flower boxes overflow from windowsills, and shopkeepers nod friendly greetings as we pass. It feels like stepping into a fairy tale—at least, until we reach Zacharia's newsstand on the corner and I spot my own face staring back at me from the cover of a glossy magazine.

"Oh my God," I gasp, stopping so abruptly that Joe bumps against my legs.

Maggie follows my gaze and her eyes widen. "Is that—?"

"Me," I confirm, my voice barely above a whisper. "And the Duke."

The magazine is prominently displayed among rows of newspapers and other publications. The photo shows me and the Duke outside Le Petite Scone last night, his hand protectively holding mine as we stand amid shattered glass. My face is turned toward him, illuminated by the street lamps, wearing an expression I can only describe as... trusting. His eyes are on me, intense and concerned.

The headline above the photo reads in bold red letters: "THE DUKE'S NEW GIRLFRIEND?"

"I forgot. They were taking photos that night," I say, mortified.

Before Maggie can respond, a young man pops up from

behind the newsstand, his face lighting up when he sees us. He's thin and energetic, with the eager expression of someone who's just discovered a winning lottery ticket.

"Good morning, Ms. Lefevere!" he calls to Maggie, then his eyes land on me and grow even wider. "And Ms. Orange!" Zacharia adds timidly, then gestures toward the magazine. "Have you seen today's Royal Watcher? You're the talk of the village, Ms. Orange!"

Joe sniffs at the newsstand, nudging a stack of newspapers with his massive nose. I tug gently on his leash, pulling him back. "I can' see that, Zacharia," I frown, upset at the picture they've chosen. In the photo, my hair is a mess, my face coated in soot. "You couldn't have picked a better moment?"

Zacharia ignores me, bending down to pet Joe. "Everyone's talking about you! The Duke's new girlfriend and her giant dog— it's the most exciting thing to happen in Atwood since the murder at the castle over summer!"

I wince at the "girlfriend" label. "I'm not—we're not—"

"Can we see a copy?" Maggie interrupts smoothly, already reaching for her wallet.

"Of course! On the house for you ladies," Zacharia insists, grabbing a copy and handing it over with a flourish.

Maggie takes it and opens to the article inside, holding it so we can both see. Joe sits patiently at my feet, though his ears perk up at a passing bicycle.

"'Duke of Atwood Finds Love with American Commoner and Animal Expert,'" Maggie reads aloud, her voice trembling with suppressed laughter. "'Sources close to the castle say His Grace has been spotted numerous times in the company of Rebecca Orange, recently hired to oversee the Duke's menagerie...'"

"*Menagerie* is a strong word…"

"The article says you saved his life during a targeted attack," Zacharia says eagerly, leaning over the newsstand. "Is it true the assassin was after the Duke because of the missing Crown Jewels?"

"Assassin? What? No!" I sputter. "It wasn't—there wasn't—"

"The press always exaggerates, Zacharia," Maggie says calmly, flipping through the magazine. "You know how it is."

"But you were there," he presses, looking at me with expectant eyes. "You and the Duke were having a romantic dinner when—"

"It was just coffee," I correct him, feeling my face grow hot. "And it wasn't romantic. We were discussing work."

Zacharia's expression turns knowing. "That's not what it looks like in the photo. The way he's holding your hand..."

I glance down at my bandaged hand, remembering the warm pressure of the Duke's fingers, how he'd insisted on helping me even though he'd been in potential danger himself.

"He was checking my injuries," I explain, though the words sound weak even to my own ears.

"Mmm-hmm," Maggie hums beside me, still examining the magazine. "Oh look, there's a whole section about your background. 'The mysterious American who captured the Duke's heart.' They even found a photo of you from the San Diego Safari Park website."

"Let me see that," I groan, taking the magazine from her.

Sure enough, there's an old publicity photo of me with a baby giraffe from three years ago. The caption reads: "Orange has extensive experience handling exotic creatures, but is a commoner prepared for life among royalty?"

Joe whines softly, sensing my distress. I scratch him behind the ears to reassure him.

"Everyone's wondering if it's serious," Zacharia says, clearly delighted to be discussing royal gossip with the subjects themselves. "Rodrigo always said royals dating commoners is the best for business. Sells twice as many magazines."

I hand the magazine back to Maggie, trying to maintain my dignity. "This is ridiculous. They've made something out of nothing. It wasn't a date," I insist, though my voice lacks conviction. "We were talking about the security concerns for the new animal exhibits."

"At his favorite bakery, after hours?" Zacharia raises an eyebrow.

Even Maggie rolls her eyes, signaling I've picked the lamest excuse ever.

Zacharia leans forward eagerly. "The article says you're the first woman he's been photographed with since his broken engagement to Lady Harriet five years ago."

"Who's Lady Harriet?" I ask before I can stop myself.

Zacharia's eyes light up at the chance to share more gossip. "Oh, she was from an old Monrovian family. Very proper, very traditional, Royal bloodline from Denmark. Everyone thought they were perfect together, but then—"

"Zacharia," Maggie interrupts gently. "Perhaps Ms. Orange would prefer to learn about the Duke's past from the Duke himself."

I shoot her a grateful look, though my mind is now filled with questions about Lady Harriet and why their engagement ended. *She was a Royal,* I think. *The kind of person a Duke should be dating.*

"Of course, of course," Zacharia says, not at all deterred. "I hope when the Duke sees the magazine he isn't too upset over it. Although, I assume he's used to his privacy being invaded."

The thought of the Duke seeing that headline and photo makes my stomach flip. What will he think? Will he be embarrassed?

"Can I buy all your copies?" I blurt out.

Zacharia blinks in surprise. "*All* of them?"

"Yes," I say firmly. "Every single one."

Maggie laughs. "Rebecca, there are at least twenty copies there. And that's just one newsstand."

"I don't care," I say stubbornly. "How much, Zacharia?"

He looks conflicted. "Ms. Orange, I couldn't possibly... "

I feel my shoulders slump. "Right. Of course. Sorry, that was silly of me."

"Don't worry," Maggie says, patting my arm. "These things blow over quickly. Next week they'll be focused on some other royal gossip."

"I suppose," I sigh, then look at Zacharia. "I'll just take one copy, then. Might as well know what they're saying about me."

As we walk away from the newsstand, Maggie nudges me with her elbow. "So... the Duke's new girlfriend, huh?"

I groan. "Please don't start."

"I'm just saying, there are worse things than having a handsome Duke interested in you."

"We don't know that he is," I point out. "And even if he were, I'm here to do a job, not get involved in a royal romance."

"Why not both?" Maggie asks innocently.

Joe trots between us, his ears perked forward as if he's following our conversation with interest.

"Not helping, Joe," I mutter, and swear I see him give me a doggy grin.

"You know," Maggie says more seriously, "at the end of the day, the Duke is just a person. Just a person who wants things that feel real. Like you and me."

As we turn the corner toward the museum, I can't help but wonder what the Duke will say when he sees that magazine. And why, despite my embarrassment and protests, there's a small part of me that hopes Zacharia is right about the Duke's interest being more than professional.

Joe bumps his massive head against my hand, as if to say

he knows exactly what I'm thinking. For a dog who can't speak, he's remarkably perceptive.

"Come on, you two," Maggie calls, already several steps ahead. "We've got a museum to investigate and a thief to catch!"

With a gentle tug on Joe's leash, I push thoughts of dukes and dating to the back of my mind and focus on the task ahead.

THE ROYAL HERITAGE MUSEUM buzzes with pre-opening energy as Maggie, Joe, and I push through the heavy wooden doors. Staff members scurry about, hanging banners and adjusting displays while I try not to let my eyes linger too long on the empty case where the crown jewels used to be. Joe sticks close to my side, his massive frame causing a few of the workers to do double-takes. I can't blame them—a 250-pound Tibetan Mastiff isn't exactly what you expect to see at a royal museum exhibition.

"Remember, Joe, best behavior," I whisper. He glances up at me with those soulful eyes that seem to say, *"I'm always well-behaved, thank you very much."*

The museum's ancient stone walls stand in stark contrast to the modern display cases and fresh banners proclaiming "The Royal Heritage of Monrovia: A Journey Through Time." Despite the theft, they're moving forward with the opening. Determination or desperation? I'm not sure which.

Maggie checks her tablet, tapping through what I assume is a very organized to-do list. "The Duke is really hoping we can salvage something positive from this situation," she says, voice low enough that only I can hear. "The museum means a lot to him—bringing royal history to the people and all that."

"I get it," I nod, watching as a young man carefully adjusts a spotlight to illuminate a tapestry depicting some ancient royal hunt. "But displaying everything except the star attraction is going to be... awkward."

"Like advertising Jurassic Park after all the dinosaurs have escaped," Maggie quips, and I can't help but smile. Her ability to find humor in crisis is one of the many reasons I've come to appreciate her in the short time I've been here.

Before we can continue our conversation, a sharp voice calls out from across the room.

"Maggie! There you are!"

Lauda strides toward us, her long brown hair bouncing with each determined step. Her glasses catch the light as she approaches, clipboard clutched to her chest like a shield.

"I was beginning to think you'd forgotten our appointment," Lauda says, her smile not quite reaching her eyes as she glances at Joe and me. "We have so much to discuss before tomorrow's opening." I can't help but notice that Lauda is, for lack of a better word— *beaming*. She looks positively pleased to be approaching the museum's grand opening, even without the Crown Jewels.

"I wouldn't dream of it," Maggie replies, her professional tone seamlessly replacing our friendly chat. "Rebecca is helping me today."

Lauda's posture shifts subtly. "Oh yes, the animal expert." She gives me a quick up-and-down glance that makes me feel like an exhibit she's considering relegating to storage. "Any progress on finding our missing treasures?"

"We're exploring several possibilities," I say carefully. No need to mention we're basically at square one.

"Well, the press has been absolutely relentless," Lauda says, her tone shifting to something that sounds suspiciously like pride. "I've done three television interviews just this morning. Channel 5, the Monrovian Morning Show, and even that streaming news service that all the young people watch."

I notice how her eyes light up as she rattles off media outlets, how her shoulders straighten and her chin lifts. For someone supposedly devastated by the theft of priceless artifacts under her care, she seems... invigorated.

"The theft has actually generated quite a buzz around the opening," she continues, adjusting her glasses. "We're expecting double our projected attendance now. Everyone wants to see the museum where the famous jewels were stolen."

"That's... fortunate," I manage, trying to keep my face neutral.

"Isn't it? Of course, I'm devastated about the jewels," she adds quickly, though her expression doesn't match her words. "But if we have to find a silver lining, the publicity has been extraordinary. I've been able to highlight the other magnificent pieces in our collection that might have been overlooked otherwise."

Joe makes a soft huffing sound beside me that perfectly captures my feelings on the matter.

"Yes, well," Maggie interjects smoothly, "the Duke is still quite concerned about recovering the jewels. They're irreplaceable family heirlooms, after all."

"Of course, of course," Lauda nods, but I can tell her mind is already elsewhere. "Now, Maggie, we need to discuss the castle's meet and greet display. I've rearranged the entire east wing to accommodate it, and I need your approval on several details."

She turns to me, as if just remembering I exist. "You're welcome to look around while we handle the administrative matters. Just please keep your... *companion* away from the displays." She eyes Joe with thinly veiled concern. "Some of these artifacts are thousands of years old, and frankly, I'd rather not have them disturbed by a dog."

Joe sits perfectly still, the picture of canine dignity, making Lauda's comment seem even more ridiculous.

"Joe is fully trained and certified," I say, unable to keep a hint of ice from my voice. "He works with rhinos and elephants without incident. I think he can handle being near some glass cases."

Lauda gives a tight smile. "Now, Maggie?"

She gestures toward the other side of the museum, clearly ready to whisk Maggie away. Maggie gives me an apologetic look.

"I'll catch up with you in a bit," she says. "If you notice anything... interesting, text me."

"Will do," I nod, watching as Lauda practically drags Maggie toward the east wing, already launching into a monologue about display lighting and informational placards.

As they disappear around a corner, I look down at Joe. "Let's get started?"

Joe's tail wags once, which I take as agreement.

I wander deeper into the museum, taking in the preparations. Workers are everywhere, polishing display cases, hanging informational signs, and setting up velvet ropes to guide visitors. The empty case where the Crown Jewels should be sits in a place of honor, now surrounded by enlarged photographs of the missing treasures with dramatic lighting that only emphasizes their absence.

"That's a choice," I mutter to myself. Rather than downplaying the theft, they're highlighting it. I'd bet money that was Lauda's decision.

I pause near a group of workers unboxing promotional materials— glossy programs with "The Crown Jewels of Monrovia" emblazoned across the front. Inside, beautiful photography of the jewels fills the pages. The marketing materials were clearly printed before the theft, but no one seems to be in a hurry to hide them away. Instead, they're being prominently displayed on a table near the entrance.

"Souvenir programs, five euros each," one worker explains to another. "Curator says they'll sell like hotcakes now that the jewels are gone— collectors' items, she called them."

Joe nudges my hand with his nose, and I scratch behind his ears absently, my mind working.

"C'mon, Joe," I say quietly. "Let's take another look at where those jewels were kept."

We slip past the workers, moving deeper into the museum toward the scene of the crime. As we walk toward the empty display case, I can't help but notice how the ancient monastery's austere beauty contrasts with the modern exhibition elements. Stained glass windows cast colored light across stone floors worn smooth by centuries of footsteps.

The display case sits on a raised platform in what was once the monastery's chapel. Tall, arched windows filter sunlight through ancient stained glass, casting colorful patterns across the stone floor. The museum staff has installed state-of-the-art lighting to highlight the now-absent jewels, creating an almost theatrical spotlight on the empty velvet cushions.

I've been here before, of course, right after the theft was discovered, but discovered nothing but a sunflower seed. The perfect crime, as they say in the movies. But my two decades of animal training have taught me one thing: there's no such thing as perfect. Every creature leaves traces. Every action has consequences. You just need to know where to look.

"Okay, Joe, let's try something different," I say, kneeling down to his level. I removed the sunflower seed we found at the case and hold up to Joe allowing him to sniff. Once he's identified the scent, I give the command: "Find."

It's a simple command but one we've practiced extensively. Joe isn't a trained police dog, but he has an exceptional nose and an uncanny ability to detect changes in his environment. I watch as he begins a methodical sweep of the area, his nose working overtime, his massive paws moving silently across the stone floor.

While he works, I run my hand along the back of the display platform, feeling for any irregularities. Nothing. It's a simple case that doesn't appear to have been tampered with.

My gaze drifts to the ancient stone walls surrounding the display. The museum designers incorporated the monastery's original architecture into the exhibition, preserving the historic character while adding modern security features. The juxtaposition is striking—centuries-old stonework housing contemporary technology.

Joe has moved away from the display case and is now sniffing intently along the wall to the right of the platform. His behavior catches my attention. When Joe focuses like this, he's usually onto something.

"What've you got, buddy?" I ask, moving to join him.

The wall here is partially hidden in shadow, away from the dramatic lighting focused on the display case. As I get closer, I notice something I missed during our previous investigation—a carving in the stone, about waist-height. It's small and weathered, easily overlooked unless you're specifically examining this section of wall.

I trace my fingers over the carving. It's some kind of symbol—a circle with intersecting lines creating a geometric pattern within. The edges are worn smooth with age, suggesting it dates back to the monastery's original construction.

"How did I miss this before?" I wonder aloud.

As my fingers move across the ancient carving, a strange sensation washes over me—a feeling of familiarity so strong it makes me pause. I've never been interested in ancient symbols or monastery architecture, yet something about this carving resonates with me on a level I can't explain. It's like déjà vu, but stronger, more insistent.

I lean closer, studying the symbol. Is it religious? Decorative? Or something else entirely? I wish I knew more about the monastery's history.

"This reminds me of something," I whisper, though I have no idea where or when. The feeling is like trying to recall a dream upon waking—the harder I chase the memory, the faster it slips away.

Joe whines softly beside me, sensing my confusion. I scratch behind his ears reassuringly.

"It's okay, boy. Just a weird feeling."

I take out my phone and snap several photos of the carving, making sure to capture it from multiple angles. Maybe Maggie would know something about it, or could point me toward someone who might.

As I'm photographing the symbol, Joe's attention shifts. He moves a few paces away, nose twitching, and begins pawing gently at a crack in the stone floor. I've learned never to ignore Joe when he's showing interest in something, so I pocket my phone and join him.

"What is it?"

I kneel beside him, running my fingers along the crack. It's one of many in the ancient floor, worn by centuries of use and the settling of the building. But as I inspect more closely, I notice something glinting in the narrow space.

Using my keys, I carefully scrape at the crack, dislodging several small, oval-shaped objects. They tumble onto the stone floor with tiny clicks.

Sunflower seeds. Just like the ones we found outside the museum grounds after the theft.

I sit back on my heels, staring at the seeds. They're ordinary, the kind you'd buy at any convenience store or supermarket. But finding them here, in this specific location, can't be a coincidence.

"Good boy, Joe," I say, giving him a grateful pat. "Very good boy."

I take an evidence bag from my pocket and carefully

collect the seeds. They're dry and appear to have been here for a while—possibly since the night of the theft.

Standing up, I look between the ancient symbol on the wall and the spot where we found the seeds. They're only a few feet apart. Connected somehow? My gut says yes, though I can't explain why or how.

The symbol nags at me. Why does it feel so familiar? I trace it again with my fingertips, trying to jog my memory. The carving is worn but distinctive—a circle with internal geometric patterns that might represent... what? The sun? A flower? Some kind of map?

I step back, trying to see the bigger picture. This wing of the monastery housed monks centuries ago. They carved this symbol for a reason. And now, in the exact same space, priceless jewels have been stolen, with sunflower seeds left behind.

I pull out my phone again and text Maggie:

"Found something interesting. Ancient symbol carved into wall near display + more sunflower seeds in crack in floor. Can we get history of monastery? Specifically any info about symbols monks might have used?"

I hit send, then turn back to the scene, trying to think like a thief. How did they get in? And why leave sunflower seed shells behind—a calling card or simple carelessness?

Joe nudges my hand with his nose, his gentle reminder that we've been standing still for too long. I smile down at him.

"You're right. We should keep looking."

I take one last photo of the area, capturing both the symbol's location and the crack where we found the seeds, noting their positions relative to the display case. Evidence, patterns, connections—these are the building blocks of any investigation.

As we continue our examination, I can't shake the feeling that these two seemingly insignificant findings—an ancient carving and discarded sunflower seeds—might be key to understanding what happened to the Crown Jewels. The carved symbol especially tugs at my subconscious, like a half-remembered song or a face I can't quite place.

Maybe it's nothing. Maybe it's everything. Either way, I'm going to find out.

"Come on, Joe," I say, giving the symbol one last glance. "Let's see what else we can discover before Maggie finishes with our suspiciously publicity-hungry curator."

Joe wags his tail and follows me deeper into the museum, his nails clicking softly on the ancient stone floor.

Fifteen

LATER, the afternoon sun casts long shadows across the patio of *Cafe de Flore* as I sink into one of the red-cushioned chairs. After the morning's excitement at the museum, this peaceful corner of Atwood village feels like exactly what I need. Joe sprawls beneath the table, his massive frame somehow managing to avoid everyone's feet while still claiming most of the available floor space. Across from me, Maggie sets down her ever-present tablet with a satisfied sigh, officially off-duty for the first time today.

"I can now declare my workday *over*," Maggie announces, reaching down to scratch Joe behind his ears. "At least until someone calls with an emergency about napkin colors or flower arrangements."

"No emergencies allowed for at least the next hour," I say, watching as a server approaches with a tray of waters. "Your boss insists."

Maggie laughs. "My boss is technically the Duke, but I'll accept your authority in this case."

The server places three waters on our table—two in glasses for us humans and one in a large ceramic bowl for Joe, who immediately raises his massive head to lap at it appreciatively. The cafe staff has gotten used to my furry companion over the past few months. Now they greet him by name and bring water without being asked.

"Speaking of your boss," I say, picking up the menu, "how are the final preparations going for tomorrow's grand opening?"

Maggie's eyes light up. "Everything is finally falling into place. The display cases are all set, invitations confirmed, exhibits ready..." She reaches for her water. "Everything except the Crown Jewels of course.

"Of course," I echo, my mind flashing back to the sunflower seeds I found at the museum this morning. "But we're not going to let that spoil the evening."

"Absolutely not. The Duke has worked too hard for this." She leans forward. "You should see him, Rebecca. He's been personally overseeing every detail when he thinks I'm not looking. This museum means everything to him—the first royal collection truly opened to the public."

The server returns, notepad in hand. "Are you ladies ready to order?"

Maggie doesn't even glance at the menu. "I'll have the lavender latte and the spring garden quiche, please."

"I'll try the..." I scan the menu quickly, eyes catching on an item that sounds perfect. "The honeysuckle tea and the harvest toast with poached eggs."

"Excellent choices. And for your handsome companion?" The server glances down at Joe, who looks up hopefully.

"He's already eaten," I say quickly, before Joe can deploy his most persuasive sad eyes. "But he might appreciate a plain biscuit if you have one."

Once the server leaves, Maggie leans back in her chair and stretches. The red umbrella above us casts a warm glow over her face, making her look more relaxed than I've seen her in days.

"So tomorrow's the big night," I say.

"It really is. And despite our little jewel problem, it's going to be magnificent." She adjusts the silverware in front of her, perfectly aligning the fork and knife. "The monastery conversion turned out even more beautiful than we'd hoped. Those old stone walls with the modern lighting—it's like the past and present having a conversation."

"I noticed that when I was there this morning. The stained glass windows are spectacular when the light hits them just right."

"I got your message about the symbol in the wall, but Rebecca, I just can't place it either! There's something about it that looks familiar. It could be important but I just can't say why…"

Our food arrives, and I'm momentarily distracted by the artistic presentation. My harvest toast is a masterpiece—thick slices of rustic bread topped with avocado, microgreens, and two perfectly poached eggs that ooze golden yolk when I press my fork against them. Maggie's quiche is a colorful array of spring vegetables surrounded by a delicate pastry crust that smells of butter and herbs.

Joe's nose twitches as the aromas reach him, but he stays in his down position, eyeing my plate with only mild desperation.

"This is incredible," I say after taking my first bite. The combination of creamy avocado, earthy bread, and rich egg creates a perfect harmony of flavors and textures. My honeysuckle tea arrives in a glass pot with delicate flowers floating on top, the steam carrying a sweet, floral scent.

"So," Maggie says, setting down her lavender latte, which is topped with a perfect foam flower. "I should probably mention that the Duke will be attending tomorrow night in his finest formal attire. I personally made sure his best suit was ready."

She watches me over the rim of her cup with a mischievous glint in her eye.

"I'm sure he'll look very... duke-like," I respond, trying to sound casual despite the surprising flutter in my stomach.

"Mmhmm," Maggie hums, clearly not fooled. "And I thought you might want to know in advance. You know, so you can look *especially* nice too."

I roll my eyes. "Maggie, I'm attending as the castle's animal expert, not as anyone's date."

"Did I say anything about a date?" She widens her eyes in mock innocence. "I'm simply suggesting that when one is attending a grand royal event where one's employer—who happens to be a handsome, single duke— will be dressed in his finest, one might want to look one's best."

"You're impossible," I mutter, but I can't help smiling. "And anyway, we have more important things to think about." Joe shifts under the table, his head finding its way onto my lap. I break off a small piece of toast—without the egg—and slip it to him. "I found more than just the symbol in the wall at the museum today."

Maggie leans forward, instantly switching from teasing friend to co-conspirator. "What did you find?"

"More sunflower seeds. They were scattered on the floor, partially hidden under the edge of the display. The kind of thing someone might absentmindedly drop while they were... I don't know, stealing a priceless royal heirloom?"

Maggie taps her fork thoughtfully against her plate. "That's interesting. Very interesting." She thinks for a moment. "Have you seen any of our suspects eating sunflower seeds?"

I shake my head. "Not yet. But I'm keeping my eyes open tomorrow night. Everyone will be there, right?"

"Oh yes," Maggie sets down her fork and counts off on her fingers. "Lady Henrietta will be making her grand entrance— she's demanded a special introduction, of course. Claude will be in mourning, moping about I'm sure. Lauda the curator will be giving tours and probably stressing about every detail."

"And Bitty?"

"Where Henrietta goes, Bitty follows. Taking Instagram photos and making cutting remarks, no doubt." Maggie rolls her eyes.

"Don't forget Pepper," I add. "She'll probably be outside with a protest sign."

"If we're lucky," Maggie says grimly. "If we're unlucky, she'll find a way to get inside and cause trouble. That girl is determined to 'liberate' the royal treasures." She makes air quotes with her fingers.

Joe shifts at our feet, and I realize he's tracking something with his eyes. I follow his gaze to see a small sparrow hopping along the edge of the patio, pecking at crumbs.

"So tomorrow night, all our suspects will be in one place," I muse, turning back to Maggie. "Sounds like a perfect trap."

I NEVER EXPECTED my new job would include attending a Royal Gala with Monrovia's elite, but here I am, dressed in my only decent black cocktail dress, with Joe sitting regally beside me as cameras flash and reporters jostle for position. The Royal Museum grand opening should have been all about the Crown Jewels, but ironically, their mysterious disappearance has created even more buzz around the event than their presence would have.

The museum's grand hall looks spectacular— Maggie's outdone herself with the decoration, which dangle from the ceiling in spirals of light and silk. Waiters in crisp white uniforms weave through clusters of guests, offering flutes of champagne and delicate hors d'oeuvres on silver trays. Joe sits obediently at my side, his massive 250-pound frame drawing curious and sometimes alarmed glances from the other attendees.

"Just smile and nod," I whisper to him. "These people have probably never seen a Tibetan Mastiff before, especially not one in a suit."

Joe looks up at me with those soulful eyes of his and gives

a soft grunt that I swear means, "*I'm not the one who needs coaching on social graces.*"

"Fair point," I concede, reaching down to stroke his golden fur.

Maggie appears at my side, looking elegant in a midnight blue dress, her blonde hair arranged in an intricate braid that wraps around her head like a crown.

"You clean up nicely," she says with a grin. "Both of you. Joe looks positively regal."

"He knows it too." I smile as Joe straightens up, as if understanding the compliment. "Meanwhile, I feel like I'm playing dress-up. Animal training rarely calls for cocktail attire."

"Well, you look lovely," Maggie says, sipping her champagne. "And more importantly, you're providing invaluable assistance. Your observation skills are exactly what we need tonight."

"It's a bit strange to have a grand opening when the main attraction is missing," I say, scanning the room, hoping one of our suspects will exhibit suspicious behavior. "Where should I start?"

"Lady Henrietta and her shadow Bitty are by the stage," Maggie says, discreetly tilting her head in that direction. "The Duke is with them now."

I follow her gaze to see Lady Henrietta, draped in what must be thousands of dollars worth of designer clothes and jewelry. Even from across the room, I can see the hair extensions and meticulously applied makeup. Next to her stands Bitty, slightly less adorned but still in full glamour, holding up a phone to capture Lady Henrietta's pose against the museum backdrop.

"Perfect, Bitty!" Lady Henrietta exclaims loudly enough for her voice to carry across the room. "Make sure you get the chandelier in the shot. This lighting is divine."

The Duke stands nearby, nodding politely but looking

slightly uncomfortable. His salt-and-pepper hair is neatly styled, and his tailored suit fits him perfectly, highlighting his athletic build. Even in a room full of wealth and status, he stands out—not just because of his title, but because of the quiet authority he carries.

"There's Claude," I say, spotting the small, nervous man hovering in a corner. "He looks like he might pass out."

The Royal Jeweler is dabbing at his forehead with a handkerchief, his small eyes darting around the room as if expecting to be accused at any moment. His tailored suit seems too big for his diminutive frame, making him look even smaller and more vulnerable.

"Poor man hasn't stopped sweating since the jewels went missing," Maggie says. "It makes him seem guilty, doesn't it?"

"The opposite attitude doesn't help either," I admit, nodding across the room at Pepper, who's holding a sign that reads "DEATH TO THE MONARCHY." She's dressed in black fishnet stockings, her hair up in a wild bun.

Maggie rolls her eyes. "How did she even get *in* here?! She must have bought a ticket, and they're a few hundred euros. For all her talk of anarchy, she doesn't seem to be roughing it herself. I should have her removed…"

"No!" I exclaim, holding up a hand. "This is a good chance to observe her behavior. Besides, the Duke wouldn't want Pepper kicked out. She has a right to protest."

"She has a right to get on my nerves, too, apparently," Maggie adds. She takes a sip of her drink then glances across the room at Lauda, who's being interviewed by the press. "Lauda's been pushing the publicity so hard. I really hope it pays off."

As we observe the various players in this unexpected drama, I feel Joe shift beside me. Looking down, I see him staring intently at the approaching Duke, who's managed to excuse himself from the conversation with Lady Henrietta.

"How are my detectives this evening?" The Duke whispers, leaning in. "Any conclusions as to the guilty party?"

"Maggie and I are still working on it," I tell him honestly, glancing down at Joe. "And so is Joe, although I think he's more interested in the smell of those little pastries than the artwork, I'm afraid."

Jack laughs, a rich, genuine sound that makes several heads turn our way. "That's my guy. I notice he's famous now, and so are you, Rebecca. The latest cover of the Atwood gossip magazine is causing quite a stir."

I can feel my face turn red. *Jack has seen the picture of us on the magazine cover that was issued after the fire.* "I'm mad at Zacharia," I say honestly. "He couldn't have picked a better photo of me?"

"I thought you looked quite pretty," the Duke smirks.

I'm lost for words, but thankfully, Maggie comes to my rescue. She points across the room at Pepper, who's sitting cross-legged on the floor with her protest sign still in hand. "Did you notice Pepper is expressing her usual affection for the monarchy?"

Jack turns to glance at the young anarchist, whose sign is now being politely but firmly adjusted by a security guard to be less visible.

"Ah, yes. Our most devoted critic." He chuckles. "You know, I rather admire her commitment. Not everyone would brave a formal event in fishnets and combat boots to make their point. Free speech is vital, even—perhaps especially— when it's challenging those in power." He shrugs. "Besides, her arguments aren't without merit. There are… some things about the monarchy that need updating."

The way he looks at me makes me think he wants to say more. My heart pounds in my chest. *Is he referencing the rule about Royals being with commoners?*

Before I can formulate a reply, Maggie clears her throat.

"Jack, they're ready for your speech," she says, nodding

toward the stage where a man in a suit is looking around anxiously.

Jack sighs. "Duty calls. But I'd very much like to continue this conversation later, if you'd be amenable?"

A soft chime rings through the hall, cutting him off. The signal for the speeches to begin.

"That's my cue," he says, regret evident in his voice. "Save me a dance afterward?"

"I'm not much of a dancer," I admit. "But I'll certainly save you a conversation."

This earns me another warm smile before he turns to Maggie. "Anything I should know before I go up?"

"Just stick to the script," she advises. "And maybe avoid mentioning the jewels directly. Let's keep the focus on the museum itself, not what's missing from it."

"Wise as always," he says with a nod. "Wish me luck."

"You don't need it," Maggie assures him, straightening his already-perfect tie. "You'll be brilliant."

As Jack walks toward the stage, Maggie turns to me with raised eyebrows. "Well, that was interesting."

"What?" I ask, feeling a flush creep up my neck.

"Oh, nothing," she says with an innocent smile. "Just observing that our Duke seems quite taken with our animal expert."

"He's just being friendly," I protest, though even to my own ears, the words lack conviction.

"Mmhmm," Maggie hums skeptically. "I've known Jack for years, and 'friendly' isn't exactly the word I'd use to describe what I just witnessed." She gives me a knowing look before turning toward the stage. "Come on, we should get closer. I need to be near the steps in case he needs anything."

As Maggie heads off, I look down at Joe, who seems to be wearing his own version of a knowing expression.

"Not one word," I tell him, and he huffs in response, his golden eyes sparkling with what I swear is amusement.

Together, we follow Maggie toward the front of the hall, my mind still reeling from the unexpected turn the evening has taken.

———

Joe and I weave through the crowd, heading toward the front of the grand hall where a small stage has been set up for the Duke's speech. People part automatically for us—or more accurately, for Joe—his massive size commanding respect even among Monrovia's elite. I notice a few raised eyebrows and whispered comments, but after years of working with exotic animals, I've developed a certain immunity to being the center of attention for unconventional reasons.

The energy in the room shifts as everyone gravitates toward the stage. Champagne glasses clink, silk rustles against wool, and the low hum of conversation creates a pleasant background noise. Despite the missing jewels—or perhaps because of them—there's an undercurrent of excitement. Nothing spices up a museum opening like a good mystery, and the press is eating it up. I count at least a dozen reporters with notepads or recording devices, ready to document every word the Duke says.

"Excuse me," a soft voice says from behind me, and I turn to find Lauda, the museum curator, standing there with a polite but strained smile.

Up close, she looks exhausted but trying hard not to show it. Her brown hair is pulled back in a neat bun, and her simple dress is professional but lacks the flash of the socialites around us. Her glasses sit slightly askew on her nose, and behind them, her eyes are bright with what looks like a mixture of anxiety and excitement.

"What do you think, Rebecca?" She leans in, face flushed. "I'm so nervous about all this—"

"No need to be nervous," I assure her. "Everything looks beautiful."

"Even without the Crown Jewels?" She sighs, but there's something odd about her expression—it doesn't quite match her tone of disappointment. "Actually, between us, this whole jewel theft has been a publicity goldmine. We've had to double security just to handle the crowd tonight."

I study her face more carefully. "I guess there's no such thing as bad publicity?"

"Exactly!" She becomes more animated, her hands gesturing emphatically. "The press coverage has been non-stop. I've already had three interview requests from international news outlets. If we'd just had a normal opening with the jewels, we might have gotten a small write-up in the local paper, but now..." She lets out a little laugh. "Now everyone knows about the Monrovian Royal Museum."

"So the theft might be a good thing," I observe, keeping my tone neutral.

"Oh, I didn't mean—" She catches herself, looking momentarily flustered. "Of course I want the jewels recovered. They're priceless historical artifacts. But yes, I suppose professionally speaking, this has put me on the map in a way that might not have happened otherwise."

Joe shifts beside me, his massive head turning to look at something across the room. I follow his gaze to see Claude furiously wiping his nose again, looking even more nervous than before.

"I have to say," Lauda continues, leaning in conspiratorially, "I'm almost glad this happened now rather than two weeks ago."

"Why's that?" I ask, my attention snapping back to her.

"Well, I've been on this awful diet for the past month," she explains, patting her stomach. "Trying to look my best for the opening. If all these interviews had come when I was still five pounds heavier and stress-eating chocolates every night, I'd have been horrified. At least now I'm camera-ready."

"The diet seems to be working," I offer, studying her more carefully now. There's something about her demeanor that's setting off warning bells in my mind.

"Thanks." She beams. "I'm a nervous eater, so the diet's been tough. I can't wait to stop eating like a bird and get back to normal food. Anyway, I should go prepare to be introduced. The Duke insists on highlighting my role in creating the exhibition." She rolls her eyes but looks pleased. "It's good publicity, right? Always put a human face on a project."

As she walks away, I stand there feeling like I've just missed something important. Joe whines softly, pressing against my leg.

"What is it, buddy?" I murmur, absently scratching behind his ear as I think.

Eating like a bird.

Something about that phrase nags at me. Birds. What do birds have to do with anything? I scan the room, my gaze lingering on each of our suspects. Claude wiping his nose again—allergies? Lady Henrietta posing for yet another photo while Bitty adjusts the lighting. Pepper, still holding her sign but looking increasingly bored.

And then it hits me.

The sunflower seed that I found near the display case where the jewels had been.

At the time, I didn't know what to make of it. But now, with Lauda's comment about "eating like a bird," a new possibility forms in my mind.

"Sunflower seeds are diet food, Joe," I whisper to him, leaning down to scratch his ears. "People eat them when they're trying not to snack on naughtier things. If Lauda was eating sunflower seeds, that means the seed by the jewels could have come from her." Joe looks up at me like he understands where I'm going with the idea, and appreciates the theory.

I look toward the stage where the Duke is now taking his position at the podium, the crowd quieting in anticipation. Maggie stands nearby, giving him an encouraging nod. Lauda is moving to the side of the stage, ready to be introduced and bask in her moment of fame—fame she engineered by stealing the very jewels she was tasked with displaying.

Joe makes a low sound in his throat, sensing my tension. I place a calming hand on his head, but my mind is racing. Should I wait until after the speech? Try to find Maggie and tell her privately?

No. If I'm right, Lauda might have the jewels with her right now. Or she might use the opportunity of the speech to slip away, especially if she senses I'm onto her.

The Duke taps the microphone gently, and the last murmurs of conversation die away.

"Good evening, ladies and gentlemen," he begins, his voice warm and authoritative. "Thank you all for joining us on this momentous occasion—the grand opening of the Monrovian Royal Museum."

Polite applause ripples through the crowd.

"While we all regret the unfortunate absence of our Crown Jewels," he continues, "I believe this evening still marks an important step forward in sharing our nation's rich heritage with both our citizens and visitors from around the world."

More applause, though I notice several people glancing at the empty display case that should have held the tiara, necklace, and bracelet.

"None of this would have been possible without the dedication and expertise of our wonderful curator," the Duke says, turning slightly toward where Lauda stands. "A brilliant scholar who has—"

My idea is just a theory. But maybe if I apply pressure to

Lauda in front of everyone, I can prove it correct. This might be my only opportunity.

"Stop!" I call out, my voice cutting through the quiet hall like a thunderclap.

Every head in the room turns toward me. I feel a hundred pairs of eyes boring into me, including the startled gaze of the Duke himself. Joe stands at attention beside me, sensing the importance of the moment.

The silence that follows is deafening. Lady Henrietta's mouth hangs open in shock. Claude looks like he might faint. Pepper actually lowers her sign, too surprised to maintain her protest. And Lauda—Lauda's face has drained of all color, her eyes wide behind her glasses.

I know in that moment that I'm right. There's no going back now.

"I know who took the Crown Jewels," I say, my voice carrying through the stunned silence of the grand hall.

CHAPTER
Seventeen

THE MUSEUM FALLS silent as I step forward. Even Joe, sitting attentively by Maggie's side, seems to understand the weight of this moment. My heart hammers against my ribs, but my voice comes out steady and clear. This is it—the moment when all those years of observing animal behavior, of picking up on the smallest signals and changes in pattern, have led me to solve a royal mystery. I take a deep breath and let my gaze sweep across the expectant faces before me.

"Thank you all for coming," I begin, looking around the restored monastery's grand hall where we've all gathered for what was supposed to be a meeting about the museum's delayed opening. The high arched ceilings amplify even my softest words. "I know the theft of the Crown Jewels has been upsetting for everyone, especially with the museum's grand opening so close."

Jack—I mean, the Duke—stands off to the side, his eyes fixed on me with what I think might actually be pride. Officer Basilier has her arms crossed, clearly skeptical about what an animal expert from California could possibly reveal. Claude keeps wiping his brow with a handkerchief, his nervous energy filling the space around him. Pepper leans against the back wall, trying to look bored but watching me intently. And Lauda stands near the front, clutching a tablet that controls her impending PowerPoint presentation with white knuckles.

"The Crown Jewels disappeared under seemingly impossible circumstances. No broken locks, no security breaches, no obvious suspects. But there were clues—tiny, almost invisible ones—that, when pieced together, tell us exactly what happened."

I turn to face Lauda directly. Her face is a mask of professional concern, but I notice the slight twitch in her right eye.

"The person who took the jewels needed them to remain missing just long enough to create tension and drama, but not so long that the museum opening would be canceled entirely. They needed a story, a narrative that would make headlines—and more importantly, make a reputation."

Lauda's tablet slips slightly in her grip.

"The Crown Jewels were taken by someone who desperately needed to make a name for themselves in academia. Someone who had been rejected from multiple positions after completing their PhD. Someone who was tired of being passed over for candidates with famous publications and media appearances." I pause, letting the words sink in. "Isn't that right… *Lauda*?"

A collective gasp ripples through the crowd. Camera flashes pop like lightning, illuminating Lauda's face as it drains of color.

"That's—that's absurd," she stammers. "I'm the curator. Why would I sabotage my own museum?"

"Not sabotage," I correct her. "*Elevate.* Your plan wasn't to destroy the museum's opening, but to ensure it made international headlines—with you as the brilliant academic who saved the day."

A reporter shouts across the room. "Ms. Orange, are you also suggesting that Lauda was responsible for the fire at *Le Petit Scone*? Was that part of her plan as well?"

I shake my head. "No. The fire was set by someone else entirely." I turn toward the back of the room. "Someone who didn't want the jewels to be found at all. Isn't that right, Pepper?"

All heads swivel toward Pepper, her blue and purple hair standing out in the crowd. Unlike Lauda, Pepper doesn't attempt to deny it. Instead, she pushes herself off the wall with a defiant thrust of her chin, her eyes watering despite herself.

"I did it," she admits, her voice trembling. "Those jewels belong to the people of Monrovia, not locked up in some fancy display case where regular people can only look but never touch. But I never meant to hurt either of you!" She says urgently, looking like a scared teenager. "It was just supposed to be a note and a harmless smoke bomb to make a point. But then you knocked over the candles and—"

"You'll be arrested as an arsonist," Officer Basilier barks, already moving toward her.

"I didn't mean to hurt anyone!" Pepper cries. "It was just supposed to be a warning. I saw Rebecca poking around, asking questions and I worried she might actually find the jewels when they're better off lost. It was a prank gone wrong. It was just supposed to send a message…"

I nod. "The prank with the smoke bomb was meant to scare me off the investigation, not to harm anyone. But it escalated quickly and Pepper was too scared to come forward, weren't you Pepper?"

Pepper nods, shaking. "I didn't mean to. I didn't want to hurt anyone…"

"Unlike Lauda, who *did* hurt someone," I turn back to Lauda, who's now visibly trembling with rage. "Lauda hit Anthony over the head with a statue. One that she plucked from this very museum. She did it because she didn't want him to interfere with her plan to steal the Crown Jewels. She needed a moment alone with them."

The cameras turn back to Lauda, who clutches her tablet to her chest like a shield.

"Lauda, your plan was quite clever, really. Hide the jewels somewhere on the premises, create a mystery that would capture international attention, and then 'discover' them just in time to be hailed as a hero. The newspapers would love it. 'Brilliant young curator solves royal mystery.' It would have launched your career in spectacular fashion."

"You have no proof," Lauda whispers, but there's less conviction in her voice now.

"Actually, I do." I smile. "You see, I found something near the empty display case that puzzled me at first—sunflower seed shells."

A puzzled murmur runs through the crowd.

"You mentioned you're on a diet—sunflower seeds are a low-calorie snack that keep your hands and mouth busy. But in your nervousness while hiding the jewels, you dropped a few shells. A small detail, but revealing."

"Come to think of it," Claude says from across the room, his stutter gone in the heat of the moment. "I've seen you eating sunflower seeds in our meetings!" He points a finger at Lauda in accusation.

"So have I," the Duke adds quietly from the stage, looking at Lauda like he's never seen her before.

Lauda's face flushes. "Plenty of people eat sunflower seeds."

"True," I concede. "But when I found those shells, they were near something even more interesting." I walk over to the stone wall where an ancient symbol is carved—a small, unassuming mark that most visitors would pass without noticing. "This symbol."

I run my fingers over the carving. "Earlier this week, Maggie showed me a secret passage in the castle, and it made me wonder—what if this building, as a former monastery, had similar secrets? What if someone with extensive knowledge of medieval monastic architecture would recognize this symbol for what it truly is?"

The room is utterly silent now. Even Joe has perked up his ears, watching me intently.

"Only a scholar with your specific expertise would know that this symbol indicates a secret compartment where monks once hid precious items during times of danger," I explain, turning back to Lauda. "And only someone with access to the museum's architectural plans would know that this particular feature had been preserved during the renovation."

Lauda's breathing has quickened, her chest rising and falling rapidly. Claude has stopped wiping his brow, his handkerchief frozen midair. Officer Basilier has inched closer, her hand hovering near her handcuffs.

"Would you like to open it and show everyone what's inside?" I ask Lauda quietly. "Or shall I?"

When she doesn't move, I turn back to the symbol. "A slight pressure in just the right spot..."

I press firmly on the center of the carving. For a heart-stopping moment, nothing happens, and I worry I might be wrong in my theory. Then, with the scrape of stone against stone, a small section of the wall slides inward and to the side, revealing a dark compartment about the size of a breadbox.

Camera flashes explode around us. Reporters push forward, straining to see. Jack moves closer, his expression a mixture of amazement and satisfaction.

"Allow me," I say, reaching carefully into the darkness.

My fingers close around cool metal and smooth gemstones. I withdraw my hand slowly, revealing the glittering diamond tiara, the ruby heart necklace, the diamond ring, and the delicate pearl bracelet that make up the Crown Jewels of Monrovia.

The gasp that ripples through the crowd is almost physical in its force. Claude lets out a cry of relief, rushing forward but stopping short of actually touching the jewels. Jack's face breaks into a wide smile. Even Officer Basilier looks impressed, though she quickly masks it with professional stoicism.

"They're all here," I confirm, carefully placing the jewels on a nearby display table where everyone can see them. "Completely undamaged."

I turn back to Lauda, who has gone completely still. "You weren't planning to steal them permanently. You just needed them missing long enough to build anticipation, then you would 'follow a hunch' and discover them, becoming an overnight sensation. The brilliant academic who solved the case of the missing Crown Jewels."

Tears well in Lauda's eyes. The tablet finally slips from her grasp, clattering to the floor. "You don't understand," she says, her voice breaking. "Three years of rejection letters. Three years of watching less qualified people get positions because they had flashier résumés. I just needed one break—one chance to prove myself."

"By committing a crime?" Officer Basilier steps forward, handcuffs now in hand. "By almost *murdering* a man? Lucky for you Anthony's woken up."

"I didn't mean to hit him so hard," Lauda says, her veneer breaking for the first time. Her lower lip trembles. "I just meant to knock him out! And I never would have let the jewels stay missing," Lauda protests. "The museum opening would have proceeded as planned, just with added publicity. Everyone would have won."

"I think Anthony would disagree with that statement," Jack says quietly. "And the people of Monrovia, to whom those gems truly belong."

Lauda's shoulders slump in defeat. "I didn't think it through. I just... I just wanted a chance."

Officer Basilier moves forward, takes Lauda's arm firmly but not roughly. "Lauda Moreau, you're under arrest for attempted murder, theft of royal property and…" Officer Basilier stops to think, then adds: "Filing a false police report."

At least she's piling on the charges, I think, finally appreciating Officer Basilier. As she leads Lauda away, Jack approaches the table where the Crown Jewels now rest. He studies them for a moment, then looks up at me with genuine warmth. "Ms. Orange, it seems Monrovia owes you a debt of gratitude. Again."

"Just doing my job," I reply with a small shrug. I exchange a glance with Maggie, who nods encouragingly. Together, we reach into our pockets and pull out matching badges that glint in the light.

Cameras flash again as reporters surge forward with questions. I feel a warm presence at my side and look down to see Joe, who has trotted over to join me in my moment of triumph. I ruffle the fur on his head.

"Good boy," I murmur. "We did it."

As the questions fly and the Crown Jewels sparkle under the museum lights, I can't help but marvel at the strange and wonderful turn my life has taken. Three months ago, I was training giraffes in San Diego. Now I'm solving royal mysteries in a European castle with my dog at my side.

Claude approaches cautiously, eyeing the jewels with visible relief. "Ms. Orange," he says, his voice quavering slightly less than usual, "I cannot express my gratitude adequately. These treasures… they are more than just valuable gems. They represent our history, our heritage."

"I understand," I tell him, and I do. The same way I understand the animals in my care, each with their own needs and stories. "They'll be safe now."

Officer Basilier returns, having handed Lauda off to another officer. In the back of the hall, I notice Pepper also being detained, although in a gentler manner than Lauda. It seems Officer Basilier has left the work to her peers, simply to be able to address her real target— *me.* She looks at me with an angry glint in her eye, finger pointed toward my face. "Miss Orange. How dare you interfere with yet another—"

Flash! The sound of a camera going off makes Officer Basilier change her tune. She notices the reporters behind her, and steps toward me, putting an arm around my shoulder for a photo. "The Atwood Police department is grateful for the help the Royal Investigators offered in resolving this matter," she says, smiling like a beauty pageant contestant. Then, she leans over, whispering in my ear: "You took another win away from my department. You'll pay for this, Miss Orange. Watch yourself."

Then, she saunters away, leaving me to wonder how she plans to make my life miserable. *Oh well,* I think, smiling to myself. *If she wants trouble, I'll deal with it another day.*

Reporters continue to shout questions— cameras flash— but Jack raises his hands for quiet. The room gradually settles.

"The museum opening will proceed as scheduled," he announces. "With added security, of course. And with a new exhibit detailing the mystery of the temporarily missing Crown Jewels— and the clever work from our Royal Investigators that recovered them."

He glances at me, a private smile playing at the corners of his mouth. "Perhaps our Royal Investigators would be willing to consult on that exhibit?"

"I'd be happy to," I reply, feeling a flush of pleasure at the way he says "our Royal Investigators."

As the crowd begins to disperse, Maggie sidles up beside me. "Not bad for your third case," she whispers. "What do you think—ready for number four? I can kidnap someone if it would help. Maybe we'll graduate from solving cases to actually creating them."

I laugh, scratching Joe behind the ears as he leans contentedly against my leg. "Let's give it at least a week before the next crisis, shall we?"

But I can't deny the buzz of satisfaction running through me. Turns out, the skills I honed watching animals for decades work just as well on humans. People are creatures of habit too, leaving their own unique tracks and tells. And I'm getting pretty good at following them.

I glance over at Jack, who catches my eye and nods in acknowledgment. There's something in that look—respect, certainly, but maybe something more. Something worth exploring, perhaps.

But that's a mystery for another day. For now, I'm content to stand in this beautiful, ancient space, surrounded by the strange and wonderful collection of people who have become my new community, with my faithful dog at my side and the satisfaction of a job well done warming me from the inside out.

CHAPTER
Eighteen

THE NEXT AFTERNOON, and the sun casts golden light across the castle gardens as I follow a path of small paper lanterns. Joe trots beside me, his massive frame surprisingly delicate as he carefully avoids crushing the flowers that line our route. The Duke sent a note to my quarters this earlier today—handwritten, not typed—asking me to meet him for a picnic lunch. "To properly thank you," it said, the elegant script making even those simple words look important. After yesterday's chaos with the Crown Jewels and Lauda's arrest, I'm honestly surprised he has time for picnics, but I'm not about to turn down the invitation.

"What do you think, Joe? Is this a good idea?" I ask my furry companion.

Joe's tail wags enthusiastically, which I take as a yes. He's been unusually chipper since we caught Lauda red-handed with the Crown Jewels stuffed in her museum display materials. Maybe he feels proud of his contribution— after all, it was his sudden barking at her bag that first made me suspicious.

I round a bend in the path and spot a magnificent oak tree with a red and white checkered blanket spread beneath it. The Duke is already there, arranging what appears to be an impressive spread of food. He's dressed in casual slacks and a light blue button-down shirt with the sleeves rolled up, looking more like a regular man than royalty. My heart does a little flip at the sight.

"Rebecca!" he calls out, waving me over. "And Joe, of course. I'm glad you could make it last minute."

"As if we'd turn down lunch," I say, approaching the blanket. Joe bounds ahead of me, heading straight for the Duke, who crouches down to greet him with an enthusiastic ear scratch.

"Chef Renauld has outdone herself," the Duke says, gesturing to the array of foods. There's a wicker basket overflowing with fresh bread, several containers of salads and finger foods, and what appears to be a chocolate cake. "She insisted on preparing everything herself once she heard it was for you."

"For me?" I blink in surprise.

The Duke laughs. "After you solved the mystery of the missing Crown Jewels, I think the entire staff views you as something of a hero. Maybe all of Monrovia does. Better get used to it."

I settle onto the blanket, feeling my cheeks warm at his praise. "It wasn't exactly rocket science. Lauda was acting suspicious from the moment the museum exhibition was announced."

"But no one else noticed," the Duke points out, handing me a plate. "Not the security team, not the royal advisors, and certainly not me. You have keen observational skills, Rebecca."

"People reveal their intentions much like animals do," I admit, accepting a glass of what appears to be fresh lemonade. "Through subtle shifts in posture, changes in vocal pitch, unusual patterns of movement."

"And what did you notice about Lauda?"

I take a sip of lemonade before answering. "She was too

excited about the press involvement. A normal curator would want to delay until the security situation was resolved. But she insisted everything proceed— because she wanted the fame that came with being attached to something like the Royal Jewels being found."

"Brilliant observation," the Duke says, his eyes fixed on me with an intensity that makes my stomach flutter. "I still can't believe she thought she could get away with it."

"Desperation makes people take risks," I say with a shrug.

Joe stretches out beside us, his massive head resting on his paws as he watches us converse. The Duke hands him a slice of what looks like premium roast beef, which Joe accepts with dignified gratitude.

"I'd say he earned it," the Duke says, noting my raised eyebrow. "If he hadn't started barking at her bag, who knows if we would have caught her in time."

I smile and reach over to pat Joe's side. "He has good instincts."

"Like his owner," the Duke says, his voice softening.

We eat in comfortable silence for a few minutes, enjoying the perfect weather and the exquisite food. Chef Renauld has included her famous honey ice cream in a portable cooler, which melts perfectly on my tongue. The Duke watches me eat with obvious pleasure.

"I'm sorry our dinner was interrupted the other night," he says eventually. "Just when the conversation was getting interesting."

My heart skips a beat as I remember the moment. We had been discussing whether royalty could date commoners when the alarm about the missing Crown Jewels had sent the entire castle into lockdown.

Oh, don't worry, I think to myself. *I've only been driving myself crazy over not getting an answer to my question.*

"You never did answer my question," I point out, trying to

keep my voice casual despite the sudden dryness in my throat.

"Which question was that?" he asks, though the glint in his eye tells me he knows exactly what I'm referring to.

"Whether royalty can be romantically intertwined with commoners in Monrovia," I say, setting down my spoon. "It was a purely hypothetical question, of course. For my cultural education."

"Of course," he agrees with a smile that makes my pulse quicken. "Purely hypothetical."

He moves slightly closer to me on the blanket, his hand just inches from mine. Joe, sensing the change in atmosphere, lifts his head with curious attention.

"I could tell you the official royal policy," the Duke says, his voice lower now. "Or I could show you my personal stance on the matter."

Before I can formulate a response, he leans forward and kisses me. His lips are warm and taste faintly of honey ice cream. My brain short-circuits for a moment, unable to process that I—Rebecca Orange, animal trainer from San Diego—am being kissed by an actual Duke in the gardens of a castle.

When he pulls back, his eyes search mine. "Will that answer suffice?"

I open my mouth, close it again, and then manage to say, "I think I might need a bit more clarification on the policy."

The Duke's laugh is warm and genuine. "You know, for someone who just solved a jewelry heist, you can be adorably obtuse about certain things."

"It's different with animals," I say defensively. "They're straightforward. Humans—especially royal ones—are complicated."

His expression softens. "You're right about that. But let me try to be straightforward now." He reaches behind him toward a small leather satchel I hadn't noticed before. "How about this for an answer?"

From the bag, he pulls out something that catches the sunlight—a delicate bracelet of pearls and gold links. I recognize it immediately as one of the smaller pieces from the Crown Jewels collection.

"Is that—?" I begin, eyes widening.

"Yes," he nods. "Part of the Crown Jewels. A bracelet that many consider the least valuable piece in the collection, but which I've always thought was the most meaningful."

He holds it up, letting it dangle between us. The pearls glow with a soft luster in the midday sun.

"The King and Queen have agreed I can give it to you," he explains. "They weren't willing to part with the tiara or the necklace, of course, but this piece... they allowed me to take. Given that the story behind the jewels so perfectly matches this moment. "

"Does it?" I ask. "It seems like the story is one of tragedy—"

"Only if you interpret it that way," Jack shrugs. "So many people focus on the Queen's initial decision to reject love rather than her regret afterwards. I like to think that the Queen made the Crown Jewels the symbol of Monrovia as a statement of equality. The jewels represent the fact that all Monrovians are the same, whether they are Royalty or not. They are confirmation that love knows no bounds, and is not tied to anything but the heart. I hope, if you see that way too, you'll appreciate a rather modern edition I had made…"

He turns the bracelet in his fingers, showing me an inscription on one of the gold links that I hadn't noticed before.

"'Love knows no station,'" I read aloud.

"Exactly," the Duke says. "The legacy of these jewels isn't really about their monetary value. It's about a love that surpassed station—a love between equals in spirit. A rejection of social rank."

He takes my hand gently in his. "I believe it's high time the real message of the jewels was out in the world. The monarchy has evolved, Rebecca. We're not bound by the same restrictions that kept them apart."

My heart is pounding so hard I'm sure he must hear it. "Are you saying—"

"I'm saying that I'd very much like to court you properly, Rebecca Orange." He fastens the bracelet around my wrist with careful movements. "If you're amenable to the idea."

I stare at the bracelet now circling my wrist, pearl and gold against my skin. It's lighter than I expected, but I feel the weight of its history and meaning.

"This is— so much," I say softly, voicing the doubt that's been lurking since our first meaningful conversation.

"Yes," Jack sighs. "I'm afraid as a result of my life structure, I lack... what do the Americans call it?" He pauses, thinking. "I lack... *game.*" He laughs out loud. "My dates are formal and stuffy. And when I try to take you on a casual dinner at *Le Petit Scone*, the place is attacked with a smoke bomb, not to mention paparazzi. Even asking to 'court' you feels like such a formal offer, but I know no other way to be."

"I'm here for the courting," I say, looking down at the bracelet. Then, I add, sincerely. "Thank you. There's no one I'd rather get smoke bombed with," I tell him. Joe, sensing my happiness, thumps his tail against the picnic blanket. "I think Joe approves," I say, glancing at my loyal companion.

"Actually, that brings me to another matter I wanted to discuss with you." Jack says, scratching Joe behind the ears thoughtfully. "I've been thinking that the castle could use another canine resident. Would you help me choose a dog of my own?"

The request is so unexpected and so endearing that I feel a

burst of warmth spread through my chest. "You want to adopt a *dog*?"

"I do," he nods. "Perhaps not quite as enormous as Joe, but I've always wanted one. Growing up, royal protocol discouraged pets that weren't part of the official royal menagerie. But now that I'm in charge of Castle Atwood..."

"You make the rules," I finish for him.

"Within reason," he agrees with a grin. "So, will you help me? You're the expert, after all."

"I'd be happy to," I say, genuinely touched by the request. It feels like another way he's inviting me into his life—not just as a romantic interest, but as someone whose knowledge and experience he values.

As we begin discussing dog breeds that might suit his lifestyle, I can't help but remember Officer Basilier's parting words to me as Lauda was being escorted away: "You'll pay for what you've done."

The memory sends a chill down my spine despite the warm sunshine. I have no doubt the police officer has it out for me—she made it clear she resented my involvement in solving the case and seemed particularly upset that I had connections to the royal family. Her antagonism toward the monarchy was barely disguised.

The Duke notices my momentary distraction. "Is everything alright?"

I consider brushing it off but decide on honesty. "Officer Basilier doesn't seem to be my biggest fan. She made some vague threats after the arrest yesterday. And now I'm associated with you," I point out. "Which probably makes me guilty by association in her eyes."

"I won't let her harass you," he says firmly. "The royal family may be controversial to some, but we still have considerable influence with the police commissioner."

I shake my head. "I don't want special treatment. I just... thought you should know that there might be trouble ahead."

His hand finds mine, fingers intertwining with gentle pressure. "Then we'll face it together. You, me, and Joe. And possibly my new canine companion, who you're going to help me find."

Joe's ears perk up at the mention of his name, and he shifts his massive body to lean against both of us, as if physically demonstrating his support.

"We'll figure it out together," I say, completing his thought.

As Joe settles his head across both our laps in a gesture of contented approval, I feel a sense of belonging I haven't experienced in years. There may be challenges ahead with Officer Basilier and whatever schemes she might cook up, but right now, in this perfect moment under the oak tree, I choose to focus on the pearls around my wrist and their message:

Love knows no station.

In this perfect, simple moment— I believe those words are true.

<h1 style="text-align:center">Letter From the Author</h1>

Dear Reader,

Thank you for dedicating your time to the world of Monrovia and Rebecca Orange! These books mean so much to me, and my hope is always that what I've written gives you the chance to escape to a cozy new place.

I love hearing from readers (seriously, it makes the job so fun!). Please reach out to me anytime by visiting www.valeriebrandy.com or finding me on social media, even if it's just to say "hi" or talk about flower names for coffees. Monrovia is special because of the community there, and I love forming the same cozy friendships around my books.

You can also join my author club mailing list for free give-aways and updates on new releases.

Warmly,

— Valerie Brandy